Upside-Down
Independence
Day

A Novel by
Gregg Sapp

UPSIDE-DOWN INDEPENDENCE DAY
Holidazed – Book 3
Copyright © 2020 by Gregg Sapp

FIRST EDITION SOFTCOVER
ISBN: 1622535278
ISBN-13: 978-1-62253-527-9

Editor: Lane Diamond
Cover Artist: Kabir Shah
Interior Designer: Lane Diamond

EVOLVED PUBLISHING™
www.EvolvedPub.com
Butler, Wisconsin, USA

Printed in Book Antiqua font.

BOOKS BY GREGG SAPP

HOLIDAZED
Book 1: *Halloween from the Other Side*
Book 2: *The Christmas Donut Revolution*
Book 3: *Upside-Down Independence Day*
Book 4: *Murder by Valentine Candy*

Fresh News Straight from Heaven

Dollarapalooza
(or "The Day Peace Broke Out in Columbus")

DEDICATION

To Bill Dobbins,
a working-class hero.

PART 1

*I'm a-lookin' for a job at honest pay, Lord Lord,
An' I ain't a-gonna be treated this way.
Woody Guthrie*

CHAPTER 1

Mazie tensed her whole body. Shabazz bristled at the end of a taut leash, staring down a terrified rabbit. Mazie double wrapped the loop around her wrists and braced her feet against the curb. Strained seconds passed. Just when Mazie felt a bit of slack in the leash, and she hoped they might move on, Shabazz sprang, salivating like a famished alpha predator, toward the rabbit. The sudden lurch nearly pulled Mazie's arm out of its socket. She staggered forward and pulled backwards simultaneously. She could only trundle along behind Shabazz, trying to hold on and stay on her feet.

The dog's ferocious bark echoed across the quad, probably awakening anybody trying to sleep in on Sunday morning within earshot. The rabbit bolted into the campus rose garden, with Shabazz in enraged pursuit. Panicked by a vision of the dog ravaging through the colorful rows of delicate polyantha, floribunda, and gallica, Mazie yelled, "Shabazz, *no!*"

The dog ignored her and barreled headlong into the Friends of Antaeus College's award-winning flowers. Mazie maneuvered around a tree and managed to hook the leash line around its trunk. When Shabazz reached the extent of his leash, he yelped, and his head snapped back so hard that Mazie worried he'd broken his spine. If that crazy dog died on her watch, there'd be hell to pay from Professor Alolo. But after a few moments, Shabazz snorted and looked back at Mazie with big round eyes, as if to say that he was okay.

Even while panting for air, Mazie smiled. She couldn't help it—dogs made her smile. People, not so much.

The bucolic campus of Antaeus College was nothing like Mazie had envisioned. Even though she'd lived most of her life within a few miles of it, Mazie had never set foot in the college's home town of Golden Springs, Ohio. Because of its leftist reputation, most folks in Coon Creek referred to it as "Piss Springs" home of "Egghead College." But they were idiots. Her brother, Boog, referred to it as "where kids learn how to hate America."

Mazie had expected a campus with Soviet-style modern architecture, academic buildings made of steel and reflective glass, box-shaped residence halls, windowless computer labs, a vast pavilion with a central obelisk for communal gatherings, and functional structures like greenhouses, solar arrays, and gargantuan windmills. By contrast, on that early summer morning the grounds of Antaeus College looked like an impressionist painting. Blue wisteria and purple bougainvillea vines wrapped in helixes around an ornate trellis that adorned the arched main gate. The central pedestrian boulevard traversed verdant lawns, bordered by beds of mixed flowers, rows of stately oaks, a few towering pines, and rolling mounds landscaped with evergreen ground cover.

Mazie walked by red brick and bluish-gray limestone buildings covered with English ivy, a rotunda lecture hall with Romanesque columns at the entrance, a vaulted library with gargoyles around the roof, and a postmodern student union building that looked to her like a place where poets might hang out. Even the dormitory where she was staying during her residency—aptly named Bard Hall—had stained-glass windows in the common room. These were grand spaces for bold and profound thoughts. Mazie felt smarter just being there.

Shabazz pulled unceasingly forward, as if he was late for some extremely urgent business. Mazie had the all-too-familiar feeling of being pulled somewhere she did not want to go. She tried to remember Professor Alolo's dog-walking instructions. Shabazz, he said, did not recognize normal dog commands.

"Desist!" she called.

Shabazz ignored her. Instead, he dragged Mazie to a dirt path that led off campus and into the woods of the Golden Springs Nature Preserve. Mazie yielded to the dog's will.

The hills and forests that surrounded Antaeus College covered a vast expanse of undeveloped land. The tracts of old growth hardwoods in the protected areas were among the oldest east of the continental divide. Elixir Creek, source of the eponymous Golden Springs from which the town borrowed its name, bordered the preserve on one side, and flowed into Clifton Gorge of the Little Miami River on the other side, where legend had it Daniel Boone leapt across to escape hostile Indians. In between, the land rose to the Shawnee Knob, the highest point in the county.

Beyond the boundary of the protected areas, the patchwork of private lands on the far side of Shawnee Knob had been logged bald, then served as pastures for a couple of decades, before being abandoned and left undeveloped for more decades, so that by the year

2016 it was once again heavily wooded. Mazie knew those lands on the other side of the hill quite well. That territory was rutted with unpaved roads popular among dirt bikers and four-wheelers. In the autumn, hunters frequented those tracts, and gunshots echoed through the valleys. The narrow, brackish Coon Creek flowed through it all.

Shabazz climbed, dragging Mazie behind him like a beast of burden. The trail ended at the summit of Shawnee Knob, where Mazie had been many times, although never via this route. From Coon Creek you needed a four-wheel drive vehicle with high clearance to get there, and even then you could only drive to where there'd been a landslide in the 1990s. To reach the Knob, you had to bushwhack a hundred or so yards, then shimmy through a gap in a wire fence.

Coming from Golden Springs, though, was literally a walk in the park—on a wide mulched trail marked by yellow ribbons hanging from tree branches. Switchbacks crossed through the steep parts. Fallen debris was moved to the side. Mazie would have liked to linger and enjoy the trek, but Shabazz seemed hellbent to get to the top, so it was all she could do to keep up.

After a thirty-minute hike, Mazie and Shabazz emerged from under the broadleaf canopy and stepped into a clearing at the viewpoint. She'd looked down from this vista of the upper Little Miami Valley many times, but somehow it looked different. On a clear day like today, she could see for miles. To the southwest, Coon Creek flowed swiftly down a ridge and then spilled into the Little Miami River on the other side of the gorge. The town of Coon Creek was farther downstream, where an ice-age glacier had deposited stray boulders across the turf like junk cars. From Shawnee Knob, she could make out the ugly smokestack at the old Hercules Steel Mill and Coon Creek Stadium, where the high school football team—the Raging Coons—lost most of their games. But in her mind's eye, Mazie could see it all: the green water tower painted with a fading CC, Burl Slocum's personal billboard at the city limit, Amity Valley Memorial Gardens, the Drink Here Tavern, the Hungry Coon Diner, a boarding house with hourly room rentals, and "church row," just off Main Street, where locals had their choice of four flavors of worship, including the Coon Creek Baptist Church of God, where Mazie's family certainly worshiped at that very moment.

A bench at the viewpoint faced northeast, looking past the gorge and toward the flatlands at the confluence of Elixir Creek and the Little Miami. The pastoral grounds of Antaeus College dominated this view. Situated at a bend in the creek and accessible by a single winding road, the college stood apart from the town, but also encompassed a good part of it. On Route 68, just beyond the entrance to the college, the "Welcome to Golden Springs" sign was hand carved in the shape of Ohio out of black walnut, with stainless-steel script lettering. Next to it, a three-tiered alpine rock fountain flowed 24/7. By decree of the zoning commission, nothing in Golden Springs exceeded two stories high. Earth tones dominated the storefronts along the cobblestones of Main Street, including Firefly Candles, Happy Legs Bicycle Shop, Vishnu's Dish Vegetarian Restaurant, Far Out Freddy's Tie-Dye, Gonzalez and Gringo's Brewpub, the Give Peace a Chance Gallery, and the Unitarian Universalist Church for ALL. Even the US Post Office resided inside of a geodesic dome.

As the crow flies, only seven miles separated the two towns. Nevertheless, on opposite sides of the gorge, no direct route connected one to the other. They were equally distant from each other culturally, too.

In pursuit of God-only-knows what, Shabazz abruptly launched forward hard enough to detach the leash from around Mazie's wrist.

"Stop!!!!" she shrieked, horrified at the prospect of losing Professor Alolo's dog before the first day of class. "Heel! Whoa! Oh, goddamnit, *desist*!!!"

Shabazz screeched to a halt at a sycamore tree on a narrow side path. He sniffed it up and down as if he were trying to uproot it by inhaling. Aroused by something that he smelled, Shabazz circled the tree, squealing, and then started to hump its trunk, peeling off shards of bark with every brutish thrust.

Mazie caught up and retrieved the leash, but worried that if she pulled the dog away before finishing, he might attack her. Somehow she had the impression that Professor Alolo would want her to stand down and let the beast have his way with the tree. Watching disturbed her, though, so she lowered her head and looked at her shoelaces.

That dog really needs to get laid, she thought.

Rufus Cobb was hip-hopping to 50 Cent in his room when he heard a crash in the hallway. Until that moment, he'd thought he was alone in the dormitory. He muted the volume and went to see what was shaking.

A young woman, wearing cutoff shorts and a sleeveless tie-dye T-shirt, and with her long red hair hanging in front of her face, held an empty box, the bottom of which had just fallen out. At her feet, a disorderly heap of books fanned out as if ready for a bonfire. She looked at Rufus with pleading eyes.

"'Sup?" he asked.

"Help?"

Rufus's high-topped dreads bounced on his head as he hustled over. When he bent down to pick up her books, he glimpsed an alluring Rorschach-blot of a birthmark on her inner left thigh. He took his time gathering the books and gave them to her one at a time while she reconstructed the box.

He lifted *Capital in the Twenty-First Century* from the pile and tapped it on the cover, noting that he'd seen the same book in Professor Alolo's office.

"I'm guessing you're here for the Emerging Writers Workshop," he said.

"Yeah. Hi, I'm Mazie T."

"Yo. Rufus Cobb."

Mazie tucked the book under her arm and offered her hand to Rufus. He started to reciprocate with a fist bump but opened his hand when he realized that Mazie was soliciting a traditional up-and-down handshake. They locked hands, squeezed once, and then released. Her palm was slippery.

They stood flat-footed, facing each other, total strangers but also classmates. At a lack for anything witty or eloquent to say, as he so often found himself when speaking to a white female, Rufus opted for his default, "Wanna get high?"

Mazie said, "I don't," and then wrinkled her brow and hedged, "I shouldn't," before finally clicking her tongue and saying, "Oh, why the hell not?"

"Hey, that's what I'm sayin'. Why not? This is like being back in college, am I right? 'Xcept now we're supposed to be like all adult and responsible. I don't feel like it though, not until I'm thirty, at least. Maybe. What's responsible supposed to feel like, anyway?"

Mazie rolled her eyes. Rufus wasn't sure how to take that gesture. It could have meant "I feel you," or even "I don't know," but it also could've meant she thought he'd asked a dumb question.

They sat on folding chairs in Rufus's room. He removed a joint from behind his ear and lit it with a wooden match, which he struck using his fingernail. He offered the first toke to Mazie. The way her cheeks puffed up when she inhaled was kind of cute.

"Looks like we'd be the first two peeps from the program to show," Rufus remarked.

"I got here yesterday," Mazie said. "It's my job to walk Professor Alolo's dog."

"Shabazz? Watch out for that dog, he's so horny he'll hump anything vertical."

Mazie coughed in mid toke, diverting the smoke from her lungs into her nasal cavities, which then escaped in puffs through her nostrils.

"Sorry. I was just jerkin' your chain," Rufus said, even though he'd been serious. "But how come you're walking the professor's dog?"

"That's my job. I'm here on a scholarship, so that's part of the deal."

"No shit? I'm on the professor's discretionary scholarship too. Now I get why we'd be the first ones here. We both got special assignments to do for him for our tuition."

"Yeah. I'm his dog walker. What's your special assignment?"

Rufus opened a desk drawer to reveal a dozen baggies containing various strains of cannabis.

"No way!" Mazie exclaimed.

"True all," Rufus replied. "Technically, I'm his 'research assistant.' But for real, my job is to provide his weed."

"How did you—? Never mind. All I have to do is walk his dog." Mazie eyes widened. "At least I *hope* that's *all* he expects from me."

"Naw," he assured her. "Professor Alolo may be a freaky old dude, but he's on the up and up."

They handed the joint back and forth a couple of times. Rufus wondered if their silence meant she felt at ease around him, or if she truly had nothing to say. Either way, it relieved him when at length she asked, "So, Rufus Cobb. Poetry or prose?"

"Narrative rap is my weapon of choice. In my straight job, I teach literature to middle school students in East Cleveland."

"Really? That sounds like a thankless job."

Rufus waved his finger to cut her off. "Not so. Iambic pentameter is the original rap. It'd blow you away to see how kids go for Beowulf once they know how to read it. Check it out...." Rufus slapped a rap beat on his lap and recited:

> *Leaping and laughing, his lair to return to*
> *With surfeit of slaughter, sallying homeward*
> *In dusk of the dawning, as the day was*
> *just breaking*

Mazie smiled. "I get it."

"For real. In my hood, if not for hip-hop, there'd be no poetry. I pound out rhythmic stream-of-consciousness rants. The lit sample I submitted in my program application was a monologue written from the perspective of a suicide jumper on his way down. His life flashes before his eyes in the seconds before splattering. With his last thought, he changes his mind. Professor Alolo said it was 'poignant,' which must have meant that he liked it, because here I be."

Mazie made a face like she'd sucked a lemon. "Poignant? Really?"

"Yeah. Why?"

"That's the exact same word he used to describe my sample."

Rufus had felt rather proud of that word, as if he owned it, so Professor Alolo using it for another's work seemed like a small betrayal.

"Oh," he said, swallowing his disappointment.

Then after another couple of seconds, it occurred to him that having poignancy in common with Mazie was kind of cool, like being conspirators. Being poignant was a kind of superpower. He imagined the two of them having many poignant discussions about their poignant feelings, opinions, and—maybe, possibly, hopefully—passions. Really *poignant* ones.

"It sounds like our writing styles are similar," Mazie said. "I mostly write flash fiction, snapshots of stories, half poetry and half prose. I write in the first person about characters who can't hold a thought on any subject for more than a few seconds at a time. They tend to be perpetually dazed, frustrated, and clueless. They're like a lot of people where I'm from."

"For real? Where *are* you from?"

"I live in Columbus."

She hadn't exactly answered his question. "That's crank. Yo—we should swap out. I'll show you mine if you'll show me yours."

Mazie firmed her cheeks and bit her lower lip. "I don't...."

"Naw huh. I didn't hear myself right when I said that," Rufus sputtered. "I must be buzzed. What I meant is that we should read each other's writing samples. That's all. Get a jump start on the workshop, yo, before everybody else gets here."

"Buzzed?" Mazie said. "I'm freakin' stoned."

She chuckled, then laughed, and then started chortling rapidly; it sounded to Rufus like popcorn popping.

Her mirth was contagious. Rufus breathed it into his lungs, and it tickled like tiny feathers. He started nose laughing, which turned into a snicker, then to a snort, then to a massive har-de-ha-ha guffaw.

Mazie hiccupped and laughed with alternate breaths, faster, building to an explosive crack-up.

They laughed at each other laughing, both doubled over, elbows to knees, chests heaving. They laughed in unabashed, ungainly paroxysms of gaiety, as if they had known each other all their lives.

They heard something. "Ahem."

Rufus hugged a cushion, trying to restrain himself. He struggled to focus through watery eyes.

"Excuse me?"

Mazie's tongue hung out of the corner of her mouth, limp and exhausted.

"I beg your pardon."

Rufus and Mazie righted themselves and looked up. A slight, pale Asian man, with thin hair in a tight ponytail and a thin, patchy beard, stood in the doorway, suitcases at his side. He wore beige gym shorts and a matching polo shirt.

"Hello. I see that you've been smoking marijuana. Good! My name is Quang Nguyen. Is this Bard Hall? I'm here for the writing workshop."

Rufus opened his mouth to speak, but he caught a glimpse of Mazie in his peripheral vision, and she him, and that triggered another riotous cascade of laughter from them both.

"May I have some of that weed?" Quang asked.

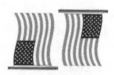

Roscoe Alolo had practiced making an entrance for two hours the previous night. He was determined to show the class from the very outset that he still had *it*. The problem was that he no longer possessed even an iota of *it* unless he got high first. Without a rejuvenating buzz, he felt old, dull, and lethargic. He could probably get a prescription for medical marijuana, but that would've taken the thrill out of *it*. He needed to feel like a renegade to act like one.

First impressions were critical. Back in his heyday, he treated every public appearance as an opportunity to make a brand statement. With his mountainous Afro, his black shield sunglasses, and his glitter shirt unbuttoned to the navel, he often made white people gasp when he entered a room. But when he read, they listened in rapt silence, either out of appreciation or fear, he never knew and didn't care.

Alas, he could no longer anticipate that his reputation preceded him, or even that every student in the class would've heard of him. He'd written his most recent book before most of them were born. It had been almost as long since he'd taught a writing class—or any kind of class, for that matter. Years ago, he'd passed the torches of his many causes to other, younger activists—or, more accurately, they'd wrested the torches from him, because he could no longer hold them and keep them burning at the same time. He had written himself out. Still, the presence of his major books in the Antaeus College library pleased him, and students had even checked out some of them in the last decade.

When the dean of the College of Arts and Sciences, Meredith Stokes, telephoned him, he answered the phone prepared to be rude. Lately, solicitors or scam artists were his only callers. His modus operandi was to answer the call and just breathe heavily until the caller hung up, which they often did angrily, as if *he* had interrupted *them*. But as soon as she introduced herself as Dean Meredith Stokes from *Antaeus College*, he surrendered all incredulity. He had to restrain himself from agreeing too quickly when she inquired if he had any interest in facilitating the summer literary residency for emerging writers. If the offer had come from almost anywhere else, Roscoe would have been suspicious. But it seemed plausible that, there, he might still be relevant. Maybe this was his comeback. Or, maybe it was his swan song. Either way, he vowed to himself that he would make the most of this unexpected opportunity.

The first meeting of the 2016 Antaeus College Emerging Writers Summer Literary Arts Residency and Workshop had assembled in the lecture hall, where they'd been told class would begin at 1:00 p.m., sharp. For them, that was. Professor Alolo would start class whenever he was damn well ready. His number one rule of making a memorable entrance was to arrive late. Tardiness not only built expectations but signaled that he was in charge. So, he waited outside in the hallway, listening. Rather than buzzing with anticipation, though, the students waited in dull silence, like timid schoolchildren. A shot of Red Bull and vodka, and he was ready.

Professor Alolo entered from the double doors at the rear of the room. The students, expecting him to come in via the door at the front, turned their heads in unison. He tapped his beechwood raven-headed cane. The students looked up and followed him with their eyes as he descended the aisle between tiered rows of seats, saying "well, well, well." As he stepped into the open space at the front of the room, he stretched his arms over his head so that his oversized African-print sweater hung over him like a tent. He'd borrowed the gesture from street preachers.

Hands on hips, he positioned himself in front of a clean whiteboard and beneath a dome of bright LED lights. This backdrop made him look black—not tan, amber, caramel, mid to dark brown, cocoa, milk chocolate, or espresso, but black as ebony, onyx, or obsidian, so black he glistened. He used white strips on his teeth so that his smile seemed separate from his face. He shaved and waxed his whole head, removing every trace of gray stubble. His wrinkles added depth to his blackness.

Professor Alolo allowed the class to absorb his aura for a moment, then addressed them, "You people are too well-behaved to be writers."

There were some half laughs and stifled groans, but nobody knew quite how to react to that statement.

The professor continued: "That must change. Nobody ever wrote anything worth a damn that didn't piss off somebody. I know you people can do it—piss off me, piss off each other, or take it to the bone and piss off yourselves. Listen up. Are you listening to me? You'd better. Before we get started, I have to disabuse you of certain presumptions right quick."

He amplified, not so much for volume, but to bring out a guttural quality in his voice that made it sound like he growled his *r*'s and spat his *s*'s. "First, you probably think you're already a pretty good writer, otherwise, you wouldn't have scored a seat in this workshop. I get how you might think so. After all, your writing samples went through three rounds of rigorous screening from hundreds of applications before the reviewers forwarded them to me, and from the somewhere around one hundred samples that I reviewed blind, I picked out just twenty. And you are the survivors of that process. Do you feel special?

"Bullshit!" Professor Alolo declared, so loud it made him momentarily dizzy. "This is your first lesson about writing—it's all bullshit. You have no idea how lucky you are that I'm here to call out your bullshit."

A Middle Eastern woman wearing a hijab and a jeweled nose stud stood and crossed her arms. Professor Alolo saw her but did not acknowledge her.

"Second, I am not here to teach you. No, you are here to learn from me. There's a huge difference. I lead, but only you can decide where you're going. I will give you my frank opinions, suggestions, criticisms, and even occasional praise. What you do with my feedback is entirely up to you. I don't have any curriculum. I'm completely okay with sitting back and doing nothing if you all come to class with no material for us to work. If you learn nothing, that's on you, not me."

The same hijab-wearing woman shuffled her feet. The whites of her eyes stood out from her dark irises and deep pupils. Again, Professor Alolo ignored her.

"Third, you are all strangers to me, as, I'm guessing, you are to each other. We all start as blank pages in respect to each other, so there's no reason not to be completely badass honest. Each of you gets a hall pass so far as everything that goes on here. For the next six weeks you all will live, work, eat, sleep, play, argue, tell stories, make love—"

Somebody in the back row of the room cheered.

"—and, above everything else, *write* together. I expect you to work together as equal members of an organic literary community. Every word any one of you writes belongs to everyone in the group. Everybody will read everything. No secrets. Get over any idea you have about privacy. You belong to me. You belong to each other. And we're all here to piss off each other.

"So, to tear down any personal barriers, for your first assignment I want each of you to write a three thousand word autobiography. It's due tomorrow."

With an exasperated huff, the woman in the hijab stomped toward to the door.

"Are you quitting already?" Professor Alolo called her out. He hoped so; it made him look more formidable if she did.

"If you must know," she huffed, "I am in need of urinating."

Roscoe Alolo grinned his trademark grin, which he had originally unveiled for his cover photo on *Mother Jones*, with his upper jaw extruding, as if to take a bite of something, his lower jaw hanging, and the corners of his lips raised so high that they pushed his cheeks into his earlobes. It made him look like a jovial madman.

He shooed for her to leave, then said, "And that, my friends, is how we do things in this class."

CHAPTER 2

Dixie snorted, circled her tracks, found a perfect spot along the fence line behind a privet hedgerow, squatted while holding her head high, and defecated copiously.

"Good job, Dix ol' girl," Toad Tuttle said to her dog.

Toad patted Dixie's rump. She put on her bifocal glasses and bent over to examine the stool; it was perfect, shaped like a miniature chocolate brain. Fashioned out of wholesome grain-free kibble, it exuded a pungent, eye-watering odor that reminded Toad of the first whiff after opening a fresh bag of cow manure.

Dixie yanked on her leash, eager to move on. Toad looked left and right, saw nobody, and took a couple of steps before sighing, "Oh, snot 'n' bother," then returned to bag the still steaming pile.

Of all the places Toad took Dixie on her daily walks, the dog liked walking around the old Hercules Steel Mill site best. She enjoyed investigating its odors and checking out what she could find in its ruins. It was like an amusement park for a dog.

Still, memories of the mill and what it had once meant for the town of Coon Creek saddened Toad. Once the mill had operated with three shifts that worked day and night. Now, only vermin and vandals visited it. A crumbling sidewalk surrounded the fenced property, and tree roots offset whole blocks in places. Bullet holes pockmarked the Do Not Enter and Trespassers Will Be Prosecuted signs by the main gate. An abundance of litter and garbage blew across the empty parking lot and gathered in heaps against curbs, lampposts, and walls. Empty beer cans filled the security booth by the gate, nearly to the ceiling. The largest pieces of refuse—kegs, a sofa, old TVs, mattresses, a couple of lawn mowers, and one vandalized VW bus up on blocks—moldered by the train tracks leading to the loading dock.

Early in the morning, the abandoned mill cast an elongated shadow over most of the block, including Toad's front yard. The old plant's brick chimneys leaned ever so slightly, as if they might come crashing down in the next hard wind. The smelters that had once contained raging hellfire were now cold and blackened with petrified soot. Shortly after the plant shut down, somebody had run a pair of soiled boxer shorts up the flagpole, and ten years later they were still there, flapping in the wind. Just about the only things the goddamned mill was good for anymore was as a place where dogs could shit, folks could dump their junk, and local rednecks could take target practice. It got uglier every year.

Back in '08, when the Hercules Steel Mill abruptly shut down, most citizens of Coon Creek, Ohio, dreamed that some benevolent entrepreneur would purchase the property and reopen it with new high-tech equipment, bringing a bounty of well-paying jobs for the next generation of Coon Creekers. After years passed and the plant remained idle, few still clung to that futile hope. Some folks started complaining that the grounds were contaminated, and they blamed unseen toxins for every malady from Sadie Hooker's migraine headaches to Ace Bragg's cancer of the colon, although back in its heyday, when the plant employed half the town, those same folks scoffed at any allegations that the rancid air inside the plant, the particulate smog issuing from its chimneys, and the greenish effluent it diverted into the Little Miami River contained anything other than healthful dietary additives.

Toad's husband, Zeke, still believed that, with the right lawyer, he could sue the hell out of those corporate bastards at Hercules, whom he was certain were responsible for his many ailments, including gout, dizzy spells, acid reflux, and erectile dysfunction. He said he wasn't greedy; he'd settle for a couple of million bucks. Too bad he couldn't also sue them for his being dumb and lazy.

Personally, Toad hoped to one day see the whole sprawling post-industrial monstrosity dynamited to bits and hauled away.

The Hercules Mill was the backdrop for Coon Creek's collective memory across several generations. Toad recalled how her grandfather boasted that the steel from the Hercules Mill built the tanks, bombers, and battleships that won World War II. When she was a girl, Toad would wait under the canopy by the main gate for the five o'clock whistle to release her father from his day's labor; he'd meet her with a grimy hug and say, "another day, another dollar, li'l darlin'." In high school, Toad often skipped classes to meet Zeke on his lunch hour, and they'd tongue kiss behind the security booth until his foreman dragged him back to work. Nearly two decades later, she had shed a tear as she watched her son, Boog, after not quite graduating from high school, fall in line to punch the time clock, with expectations of doing the same for the next forty-odd years. Such was the cycle of life in Coon Creek for over half a century. The work was brutal, but it paid a living wage. As Zeke said, "Ain't much more a workin' grunt like me can ask for." That was cold comfort to Boog, though. All that was left for him to do was enlist in the army, and Toad didn't like the way that turned out for him.

Dixie stiffened, focusing her undivided attention at a clump of dandelion weeds growing out of a pothole. Something moved in there. Toad grabbed the leash in both hands, in case Dixie made a sudden lunge. She urged, "C'mon, Dixie hon, let's get us outta here," but the dog was fixated.

Two beady eyes, a pinkish nose, and a set of humming whiskers peeked between dandelion stalks. Dixie started whirling her tail and pawing at the bars of the fence. She greeted the creature with a series of short staccato barks.

A large rat, the approximate size of one of Boog's work boots, scampered onto the rim of the pothole, raised itself on its haunches, and rubbed its paws together mischievously. Toad thought she recognized it.

Dixie crouched on her front legs. She panted so hard that just listening to her made Toad breathe harder too. If Dixie could speak, Toad imagined she would have asked the rat if it wanted to play. The rat skittered closer, inches from the fence, nearly within lapping range of Dixie's tongue.

"Heaven's to rabies," Toad exclaimed, "I think that there rat is Old Hillary." She tugged on the leash to tear Dixie away from the rodent. The dog tugged back, in apparent sport.

Disinterested, the rat sniffed in every direction other than toward Dixie. Desperate to attract its attention, Dixie continued yapping enthusiastically. Finally, the rat meandered along the fence line until it found an open manhole cover and escaped beneath it.

"Go ahead, Hillary. Ignore us. We're just a 'basketful of deplorables,' anyhow. So good riddance to stray vermin," Toad declared. She reached down to pat Dixie's head. "Let's get us home, girl. We've done lollygagged hereabouts too long already."

Dixie stuck her nose between Toad's legs and nudged her inner thighs, which was her way of making up. She then bolted in the direction of home, pulling Toad along behind her.

Zeke Tuttle knew that Toad would expect him to have dressed and readied himself for church by the time she returned home from walking her precious little princess dog, Miss Dixie. After thirty-seven years of marriage, he was well practiced in falling short of her stated expectations, and he seldom aspired to more than fulfilling her minimal unstated ones. He had gotten out of bed, splashed his face, and even brushed his teeth; that, he figured, ought to demonstrate a good faith effort.

Of course, that didn't mean that she wouldn't grouse about how lazy he was and possibly threaten to cut off his liquor allowance. Her ultimatums had no more effect on his behavior than one of Reverend Belvedere's fire 'n' brimstone sermons—which was to say, none. If she ever did cut off his booze, he had a hidden stash of rotgut bourbon in the cellar to tide him over until she either forgot or gave up trying.

Zeke didn't mind that she nagged, because it went in one ear and out the other. In his heart, he acknowledged that she was generally correct when she called him lazy, for he'd learned long ago that ambition wasn't worth the bother. Time, experience, and a bad back had disabused him of the myth that hard work and determination led to anything other than disappointment and an early death.

When Toad came through the door, Zeke was wearing boxer shorts, sitting at the kitchen table, eating microwaved biscuits and gravy, and pretending to read the newspaper, hoping to discourage conversation. Dixie, who didn't seem to get that he didn't like her all that much, scrambled across the kitchen and dove slobbering onto his lap.

"Whoa, yah ding dang dawg," Zeke grumbled, pushing back. "My back hurts."

"She likes you," Toad said. "Cain't account for poor taste."

Zeke let the insult slide. It was less grief than he'd expected for not being ready for church. To show his appreciation, he consented to let her dog drool on his knee.

"How'd her shit look this mornin'?" he asked.

"It was brown and lumpy and smelt a whole lot better than yours."

"With all that expensive chow she gets, her shit ought to smell like lilacs in the spring. Yah feed that mutt better than yah do me."

"Firsts of all, Dixie ain't no mutt. She's a purely bred American boxer. And seconds of all, she's worth a whole lot more money than you are."

"I'm a thoroughbred West Virginian. Men like me is a dying breed."

"True," Toad said. She sat down next to him and took a bite out of an apple. "But since you ain't quite dead yet, you best get ready for church. You need it."

"I s'pose you're right," Zeke agreed, retreating to their bedroom.

Toad had laid out his church clothes on the bed before leaving to walk Dixie. She'd folded and placed each garment on top of the bedspread, arranged according to the order that Zeke got dressed, starting with his drawers and finishing with a pair of ugly blue-green argyle socks, which still had a Walmart price tag stapled to them. Zeke wondered what had possessed Toad to buy him a pair of argyle socks. When did she ever know him to wear anything other than white cotton crew socks? Never. Except, that is, for his Brutus Buckeye scarlet-and-gray-striped socks, which he generally wore just once a year, for the football game against Michigan. On a whim, Zeke decided that he would switch out those argyles for his Brutus Buckeye socks and wear them to church that morning. He would loosen his belt so that the cuffs of his trousers dropped over his ankles. Then, when they sat down together in the pew at the Coon Creek Baptist Church God, he'd hoist them up to reveal that he'd defied her choice in hosiery. He was anxious to see how she'd react.

Any small victory, even if it was only over stockings, would absolutely make his day.

Strolling the packed-dirt paths and grassy lawns that crisscrossed the Amity Valley Memorial Gardens made Faye Pfeiffer feel at peace. She took the same circuitous route through those hallowed grounds every morning. Wearing her standard black suit and tie, she carried a folded flag tucked under her right arm. Her cap-toe oxford dress shoes repelled the morning dew, but the cuffs of her pressed pants and her cardigan socks were moist from ankles to shins. She was trying to break in some new foam orthopedic insoles that Reverend Belvedere said would help her plantar fasciitis, but with wet feet that squished with every step, her heels hurt as much as before, maybe more. The pain did not distract her from her duty.

In the graveyard, Faye knew everybody by their first name. Except for the oldest residents, who dated back to the nineteenth century, most of them had been her family's clients. The Life Eternal Funeral Home had been the Pfeiffer family business for four generations, serving the citizens of Coon Creek with supportive, dignified, compassionate, and affordable mortuary services. The tradition began when Faye's great-great-grandfather, a former moonshiner, patented his secret formula for embalming fluid, purchased a 1930 Cadillac hearse, and opened shop in the garage of the Pfeiffer household. The adjacent funeral home and the rolling cemetery grounds together occupied an entire block near downtown Coon Creek. When folks joked that death was the biggest business in Coon Creek, they weren't just being sarcastic.

Amity Valley Memorial Gardens never looked grander than at the start of summer, just after Memorial Day, when the greening landscape rippled with the colors of the hundreds of plastic American flags she had placed at the graves of every veteran, their spouses (including exes), and their children. That just about covered the whole population, for Coon Creek was known throughout the state for volunteering whenever the nation issued a sacred call for soldiers. After 9/11, more of the community's young men went to defend democracy in Afghanistan than stuck around in Ohio. After the Hercules Mill closed, Coon Creekers had few non-military career choices available to them. Most of the young men graduating from Coon Creek High School opted for military service. More and more young women did, too. They were lucky—Faye wished that she'd had the opportunity to enlist when she was younger.

Whatever path folks chose, they all led to the same spot. In the center of the cemetery, on a grassy mound next to a well hand pump, Faye began every new day by raising Old Glory up a tall flagpole. Rows of Pfeiffer family graves—the final resting places of dozens of Faye's proud, hard-working, God-fearing progenitors— were arranged in a semicircle around the flagpole, as if to bear witness to Faye's solemn daily ceremony. Among them was her parents' shared monument; its hand-rendered inscription read:

> *Wilbur Pfeiffer, 5/9/42 to 12/31/11*
> *Mildred Pfeiffer, 9/13/43 to 12/31/11*
> *Bound forever in love*

Faye never passed without looking at the vacant plot next to theirs where, one day, she would be laid to rest.

The folded flag that Faye carried under her arm was the first-Sunday-of-the-month flag. She had flags for each day of the month, each with its own story to tell. A lot of people gave their old flags to Faye. Louisa Carp had donated that day's flag; her husband died heroically during combat in Quang Nam Province, Vietnam, when he fell on a live grenade to save the men in his unit. Faye kissed it before fastening it to the line, hoisted it, and saluted when it reached the top.

In the evening, she would return to lower the flag and bring it home to its place of honor in her flag closet. She would never, under any circumstances, leave any flag flying after dark. It irritated her that many of her well-intentioned neighbors neglected that aspect of flag etiquette. Even though she believed, in her heart, that there was no more patriotic community in this greatest nation than Coon Creek, Faye sometimes felt that her fellow citizens took their blessings for granted. They didn't realize how lucky they were to live in America.

That was one reason why she placed flags at veterans' graves on Memorial Day, and also why, for the last twenty years, the Life Eternal Funeral Home had foot the bill for Coon Creek's annual Fourth of July "Boom-a-Thon" fireworks show. It was well known as the most spectacular in all of Greene County. Sponsoring it was expensive—getting more so every year—and a lot of hard work, but Faye shrugged it off as well worth the investment. It was important to her that the celebration was 100% homegrown. Besides, she had a passion and God-given talent for blowing things up.

The sound of church bells interrupted her ruminations. Was it 9:00 a.m. already? Time sometimes got away from her when she dreamed her American dreams. Faye tsked at herself, brushed off her jacket, straightened her tie, and then hastened across the lawn, hopping over grave sites and dodging markers, to get to the church before the service began.

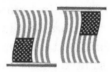

Toad chewed the fat with Edith Doody, both literally and figuratively. Sitting on a curbside bench in the town square, beside the statue of Philander Fink and across the street from the Hungry Coon Diner, the two women sampled Edith's spring batch of sweet-and-spicy venison jerky.

"Mmmmaaaahhh," Toad mumbled while chewing.

"Do yah taste that extra little bit of zing I put in it? Can yah guess what that is?"

Toad could have chewed that wad of jerky all day and still not guessed the secret ingredient. Her taste buds weren't what they used to be. She shifted the wad into her cheek so she could talk. "Well, I do alright taste something special in it. Tastes like...."

"So sauce!" Edith eagerly divulged. "I mary-nated it overnight in a bowl of that, what'cha call it, oriental so sauce."

"Do you mean soy sauce?"

"Yeah. Ain't that what I said? I got the idea from watching Rachel Ray's program, she said it was good with just about anything. Henshaw's IGA didn't have none, so I had to go all the way to Walmart in Dayton to get a bottle of the stuff."

"Maybe, since it's some kind of Japanese jerky, we ought to eat it with chopsticks," Toad deadpanned.

Edith laughed so hard that her Adam's apple shook, as if that was the funniest thing she'd ever heard in all of her life. Toad laughed at Edith laughing. Folks passing on their way to church paused to look at them, which only made both laugh harder.

"Well," Toad sighed, catching her breath. "That sure felt good. We all don't laugh enough around here no more."

An engine backfiring, as loud as a shotgun blast, interrupted their hilarity. Toad tensed her head and shoulders, and she swallowed involuntarily. A chunk got stuck sideways in her throat, making her cough and gasp for air, until the same engine backfired again, triggering a violent hiccup which dislodged the jerky. Toad spat it into the grass.

"Whoa, Mom. Are you okay?" Boog called from the window of his pickup truck.

Toad called out, "Bobby Gregory Tuttle! That bomb that you drive around in nearly turned my stomach inside out. When are you a-gonna get it fixed?"

Boog revved the engine. "Most of the time it works A-OK. It only backfires when I'm goin' to church."

"Hey, Meemaw," Justin yelled at her from the bed of the pickup, where he was sitting on a wheel well.

"Justin Zachariah Tuttle! What in the name of bejeezus are you doing in the back of that truck? Ain't no seat belts back there, that's for sure."

"Seat belts are for pussies, Meemaw."

"Shut your mouth," Toad commanded. "You're sitting right here in front of God's house, and He can hear you."

Justin looked to his father for a ruling as to whether what he'd said would bother God.

"Give the boy a break, Mom," Boog said. "He already gets enough Holy Roller crap from his mother."

Maybe if you had paid some mind to Darlene's Holy Roller crap, she wouldn't have kicked you out of the house, Toad thought. Although she could hear those words rattling around in her head and she could almost taste them on her tongue, she resisted speaking them aloud. Even so, she could tell by how Boog rolled his eyes that he knew what she was thinking. Scolding people without saying a word was one of Toad's special skills.

The engine burped and emitted a puff of black smoke that made people standing in front of the church scatter for fresh air. Justin whooped and raised his arms in front of himself, brandishing an invisible rifle and pulling off several shots. He shouted, "Bing, bang, boom."

Zeke came out of the restroom at Joe's Sunoco. He often went there to sneak a drink before church, on the obviously fabricated grounds that he suddenly needed to piss. Zeke knew that Toad knew what he was doing, and Toad knew that he knew that she knew, so she considered it unnecessary to confront him about it. She actually took it as a sign of respect that he felt like he had to sneak around.

Zeke went to inspect the vehicle. "Lift open the hood," he said, rolling up his sleeves. "Let's have us a look."

Before Boog got out of the driver's seat, the bells to the Coon Creek Baptist Church of God started ringing. Toad thanked Jesus for His timing, for she knew that once Zeke and Boog popped the hood on that beat-up old wreck, no matter what they found under there it would occupy their attention for the rest of the day. Their purpose was not so much to fix anything as it was to look like they'd tried their best before taking it to the shop. Neither Zeke nor Boog knew jack shit about mechanics, but that never stopped them from tinkering.

"The truck can wait," Toad said. "But the Lord cain't."

None of them moved until Toad swept Zeke, Boog, and Justin in the direction of the church. Once they were safely inside, she jogged up the steps, passed them in the vestibule, and then led them down the aisle to a pew in the front row. She pointed where she wanted each of them to sit. Sometimes, Toad wondered if not for her prodding them to go to church they'd even remember that Sunday was the Lord's day. If by some miracle they managed to get into heaven, they'd have her to thank.

Seeing her boys—that's how she thought of them, as her "boys"—seated side by side by side in the pew on Sunday morning pleased Toad. Still, she yearned for the one who was missing, her only daughter, Mazie Sue. As much as she was proud of her for graduating from Ohio State and getting a fancy job in Columbus, Toad still worried about whether she lived the right way. The city was a sewer of vice and temptation, where many a young person strayed into wrongdoing. Edith's eldest son, Buck, had gotten into some serious trouble there one weekend, for which he spent a month in jail and paid a fine of $5,000. Toad and Edith both agreed that in the modern world, with all its instant temptations and on-demand seductions, it was harder than ever to live a good Christian life.

As she settled into her seat, Toad cast a backwards glance, the same as she did every week, in the ardent but unlikely hope that she'd see Mazie come walking through the church doors. Just once more before she died, she longed to see her entire family gathered all together in church. It was as much a mother's job to hope as it was to worry.

Burl Slocum never missed a Sunday at the Coon Creek Baptist Church of God. He always sat in the last row of pews, so folks would pass him as they entered the church. The whole point of going to church was to be seen. Burl figured that if he didn't go to church, people might gossip, so why give them something else to talk about? In practice, he didn't necessarily believe in God or worry very much about his immortal soul. He picked and chose among God's Ten Commandments; seriously—who *didn't* lie? Maybe when he got older and needed it, he'd start trying harder to believe.

Likewise, Burl considered Reverend Belvedere to be more of a pragmatist than a dogmatist. He liked that about him—they both saw advantages in encouraging other people's faith. Religion benefited both of their businesses. It saddened and worried Burl that over the last few years the congregation had dwindled down to a core of true believers and those, like himself, who regarded church attendance as a social obligation.

During the service, Burl folded his hands and lowered his head as if praying, when in fact he was thinking about what he'd do afterwards. The only part of the service he ever paid attention to was the reverend's sermon.

Reverend Belvedere placed his hands on either side of the lectern and cleared his throat to signal for silence. Clearing his throat was an instrumental part of the reverend's homily, which not only directed the flock to pay attention, but also suggested the tone of the words that he would deliver. His throat clearing repertoire included a nasal snort for comic effect, a rolling *ahem* for a casual style, a hoarse grunt for a grave or scolding emphasis, and others for circumstances that ranged from felicitous to somber. Burl thought that he'd heard them all. That morning, though, the reverend cleared his throat in a new way, drawing air from deep within his lungs and expelling it in a slow, raspy roil, in a manner that seemed to signify that he was preparing to make some momentous announcement.

"Brothers and sisters in Christ...." Reverend Belvedere cast his gaze broadly over his flock, side to side and front to back. He projected his voice as if to address a much larger audience. "I don't need to tell you that we live in challenging times. Coon Creek has endured more than its share of hardship and strife. There's not a single person here today who has not felt loss, grief, frustration, fear, and even despair on behalf of themselves, their families, or their neighbors. It is painful, and, yes, I know that it can try a person's faith. Even my faith.

"But faith is *supposed* to be hard. Nobody ever said that getting into heaven would be easy. Jesus taught us that 'Not everyone who says to Me, Lord, shall enter the kingdom of heaven, but he who does the will of My Father.' Still, it seems that every time things start to look a little better for us hereabouts, something happens to squash our hopes, like we are mere bugs under Satan's hooves.

"To those of you who struggle to find meaning, though, remember that Jesus is your best friend, who will always listen to your prayers, day or night, whenever you drop onto your knees and call for Him.

"We are all sinners. I am, too, just like you. Maybe a sinner with better intentions, but a sinner, nonetheless. God tests my faith, same as he does yours. Fortunately, God's test is open book, and the name of that book is the Bible. And what does the Bible tell us to do?"

Reverend Belvedere paused to give anybody who felt so inclined a chance to respond to that question. Nobody did. Burl had heard this spiel often enough to know that the correct answer was *to pray*, but he wasn't about to upstage the reverend by saying it out loud.

The reverend fulminated, "*He tells us to pray!* Only through sincere prayer does God reveal His intentions. We must humbly seek His guidance, for as Mark assures us, 'Whatever you ask for in prayer, believe that you have received it, and it will be yours.' Let me tell you about a conversation that I had with Jesus just the other day.

"So, recently, when I was aggrieved after losing my dearest Maude—God rest her soul—that's exactly what I did. I prayed nonstop for an entire day. I prayed before I got out of bed in the morning. Instead of drinking my usual wake-up cup of coffee, I prayed. I set aside all my pressing affairs for that day, closed the door to my office, and just prayed, prayed, and prayed some more. I prayed so hard that it made me sweat. I clasped my hands together so tight that my finger joints ached. My back began to hurt, but I prayed through it. Nothing distracted me—not dogs barking, not horns honking, not cars backfiring, not ambulance sirens, not even when my daughter knocked at the door to my office and asked if I was still alive. I kept praying with all my might, determined that I would not stop until I got an answer. I prayed to God—What is Thy will for me?

"It was late at night. I was exhausted and sore all over my body, but I resisted the urge to sleep. Finally, I felt my soul rising right out of my body. I heard a voice. It said to me just two words: *Do it!*"

Reverend Belvedere opened his arms, palms up, in a come-to-Jesus gesture.

"And then I knew what He wanted from me. So, I hereby today announce in front of you all, my dear brothers and sisters in Christ, that I can no longer stand by idly and watch our beloved town degenerate into ruin, vice, and perfidy. God calls on me to act. Therefore, I intend to run for the position of mayor of Coon Creek."

Burl thought he must have heard wrong. Reverend Belvedere hadn't said a word to him about it! Normally, the reverend would have run that idea by him first. It was all well and good that he thought he'd heard God tell him what to do, but still Burl deserved the courtesy of being consulted, as well.

The congregation was absolutely dumbfounded. They looked down or from side to side, anywhere other than at the reverend. In the ensuing silence, Burl felt like everybody was holding their breaths. Reverend Belvedere walked around the lectern, stood at the foot of the altar, and widened his eyes, as if to say — *say something, for crying out loud.*

Finally, recognizing an opportunity to burnish his born-again credentials, Burl Slocum pushed off the back of his seat to stand, all 350 pounds of him, tugged on his suspenders, and bellowed, "You have my vote, reverend."

This opened the floodgates for further affirmation. "Mine, too," Faye Pfeiffer concurred.

"And ours," Gertrude Tuttle said, speaking for her entire clan.

Reverend Belvedere was so relieved that he started to weep. "Bless you," he said. "Now let's sing a hymn of joy. How about 'Jesus, I Come'?"

CHAPTER 3

Meredith Stokes, dean of the College of Arts and Sciences at Antaeus College, was grateful and honored, sure, but mostly relieved when Roscoe Alolo accepted a one-year visiting scholar appointment and agreed to serve as director of the 2016 Antaeus College Emerging Writers Summer Literary Arts Residency and Workshop. The trilogy of dystopian novels — Impossible to Underestimate, Defenders of Virginity, and Head in Search of a Brain — that he wrote during the 1970s had been very popular at the time. They were perhaps most famous for being thrown into the fires at innumerable Reagan-era book burnings. For that reason, as much as for their literary value, they had influenced a whole generation of young activists. Above all, Meredith needed his quasi-celebrity appeal to satisfy the board of directors that she could deliver on her promise to attract big names to Antaeus College.

In Meredith's first year at the college, after a series of cancellations and apologetic refusals from several somewhat prominent writers, she'd worried she might have to cancel the whole summer writing program before she finally recruited a friend who owed her a favor: Francesca Pembroke, author of the self-published Hergasm series of erotic lesbian steampunk science-fiction novels. Meredith had read them all, and although she loved them, she had to admit they weren't for everybody. During the first class, Madame Pembroke advised her students to always masturbate before writing to get into the mood. Upon hearing about this recommendation, one elderly donor to the college remarked to Dean Stokes, "Personally, I don't have anything against masturbation, but I don't think that it should be part of the curriculum."

Meredith promised to do better next year.

That was not an easy promise to keep. Due to sinking enrollments, budgetary shortfalls, and programmatic cuts, Antaeus College's status as a hot literary destination had declined in recent years. Try as she might, she could not entice any A-list writer to commit to the program. Although more contrite about refusing her, B-listers were also reluctant. Desperate, she scoured the literature section in the library, searching for ideas. There, she stumbled across the name "ALOLO" on the spines of a row of dusty books. Roscoe Alolo? Hmmm. Back in college, she'd read his books in a graduate course in Structural Dissent in American Literature. But was he even still alive?

It took several calls and emails to confirm that indeed he was. When she contacted him to ask if he would direct the program, he seemed suspicious, but didn't say no. Meredith used pie to persuade Roscoe to come to Antaeus College. It was a hunch. Pie imagery and symbolism figured prominently in Alolo's body of literature. In *Impossible to Underestimate*, the falsely-accused main character requested sweet potato pie for his last meal before being executed by stoning; the long suffering heroine of *Defenders of Virginity* got her revenge on God when she seduced the Messiah by serving him a hot, gooey wedge of cherry pie; and, perhaps most notably, on the final page of his PEN

Bellwether Prize-winning book, *Head in Search of a Brain*, the leader of the slave revolution administered justice by smooshing a banana cream pie into his former master's face. Dean Stokes gambled that Alolo's fondness for pies was more than just a literary device, and that he loved pies on his plate as much as in his books.

So, at a reception in his honor, Meredith presented him with a locally baked, blue-ribbon-winning pecan pie that folks drove from as far away as Louisville or Indianapolis to procure. She crossed her fingers and assured him that it would be the best pecan pie he'd ever tasted. It was. One bite and he was hooked. High on pie, he not only agreed to direct the summer residency program, but also consented to represent the college at the Golden Springs Independence Day Festival of Lights. All he asked in return was a scoop of vanilla ice cream.

On the evening after the first day of class, Meredith went to the alumni house, where Professor Alolo was living, to check on him and see how it had gone. She found him chest deep in the refrigerator, mumbling "mmmmwf" and "aaaahump" to himself.

She knocked on the wall. "Professor Alolo?"

Roscoe raised his head above the refrigerator door. He popped a peeled kiwi into his mouth, shifted it to his cheek, and said, "Call me Roscoe."

Meredith watched the kiwi pass down his esophagus; it looked like he'd swallowed it whole. "I didn't mean to interrupt," she apologized.

"No worries. If you were interrupting, I'd just ignore you. Nothing personal—but if I didn't ignore people, I'd never get anything done."

Shabazz, who'd been dozing on an embroidered sofa in the parlor, awakened and flew across the room at Meredith, jamming his nose into her crotch. He flapped his tongue, and drool rained from side to side. She tried to shield herself with her purse.

"Shabazz! Desist!" Roscoe commanded.

Shabazz continued to slather Meredith's thighs with sloppy kisses, leaving a conspicuous wet mark on her slacks between the legs.

Roscoe grabbed the dog by the collar and pulled him, nails scraping the floor, into the pantry and shut the door behind him. Shabazz pawed at the door and whined to be let out.

"Sorry," he said to Meredith. "Shabazz is horny."

Meredith had thought it peculiar when Professor Alolo made bringing his dog a condition of accepting the residency, and even though having a dog clearly violated the alumni house's policy, she approved it under loose interpretation of an allowance for service animals.

"Not at all. I love dogs," she lied. "But I just came by to ask how your first class went."

"I'm hungry," Roscoe said, patting his belly.

"Oh?" Meredith shrugged off the abrupt change of subject. "Well then, let's grab a bite to eat. There's a vegan restaurant I really like in downtown Golden Springs."

"Where can you get those scrumptious pecan pies? I've been craving a piece ever since I got here."

"Uh, not in Golden Springs."

"Where, then? I'll skip dinner and go straight to dessert."

"Sure. No problem," Meredith said, mentally rearranging her evening's schedule. "Pie is the specialty at a diner in a small town not far from here. It's kind of a roundabout trip to get there, though. It takes about half an hour to drive."

"Thirty minutes," Roscoe repeated and rolled his eyes, as if recoiling from the inconvenience. "Then we should leave now. Do you mind driving?"

"I suppose. I mean, sure. My Smart car is all charged up, so we should be able to make it there and back."

"Then let's go. I'm very hungry."

Burl Slocum sat in a lawn chair, admiring his handiwork. Actually, Justin did all the work, but the project was entirely Burl's idea. It looked righteous, all right. It still lacked something, though.

"It needs more than just a question mark. Add an exclamation point, then put another question mark at the end," he instructed.

On the catwalk in front of the billboard, Justin rummaged through the assorted characters in a box he'd dragged up there until he found the prescribed punctuation marks. He suctioned each in turn onto the end of a letter-changer pole, stood on a step stool to reach the line of text, and then placed them as Burl had indicated.

"How's that?" Justin asked.

Burl was proud of his billboard. It was the first thing drivers approaching from the west via State Route 343 saw when they hit Coon Creek city limits. For years his father had leased that billboard to Edith Doody—his father always had a sweet spot for Edith, or maybe just for her pies. The billboard had depicted a raccoon wearing a bib, gazing at a slice of apple pie, and licking its chops, with a caption that read, "Keep your eyes on the pies. Hungry Coon Diner, serving hungry coons since 1975." When the old man died, though, Burl had revoked Edith's billboard privileges; he had his own idea about what to do with it.

Burl Slocum owned six hundred acres outside of town, including a parcel of land in a pasture along the state route, where the dominant feature on the landscape was his billboard. It rose at a bend in the road above a barbed wire fence, so as drivers rounded the curve it appeared smack dab in front them. When they saw it, drivers often slammed their brakes, thinking the billboard was closer than it actually was, and that if they didn't stop immediately, they'd crash through it. Burl liked that, for it all but ensured they *had* to read it. The billboard was his soapbox to stand on, from which he could promulgate his unfiltered ideas and opinions.

Burl had lots of opinions: the best opinions in Coon Creek, in his own opinion. The billboard was a perfect canvas for his wit, warnings, and proclamations. Some years ago he'd purchased a life-size cutout of Uncle Sam from an army surplus store. With a little acrylic finish, super glue, and suction cups, he rigged old US so that he stood proudly in the corner of the billboard, his hand extended with a finger pointing to whatever patriotic words of wisdom Burl felt inclined to display there. Often, he borrowed popular slogans like "Your mother was pro life," "When they pry it from my cold dead fingers, that's when I'll give up my gun," and "My kid beat up your black gay Muslim honor student." He fancied that his pithy, eye-catching catchphrases might stick in somebody's head and—*maybe*—change some minds.

Hence, playing off a currently popular rallying cry of that summer, his latest billboard testimonial read, "What about Make American Great Again don't you understand!?!"

"Howzit look now, Mr. Slocum?" Justin shouted down from the catwalk.

Burl closed his eyes tight, then snapped them open suddenly to simulate the impression that a driver would get when rounding the bend.

"Hmmm," he pondered. "How about spelling out the word GREAT in all capital letters?"

"Whatever you say, boss."

Burl believed that his billboard performed a public service by exposing the un-American activities of so-called intellectuals and their lackeys in the media, the arts, and even in professional sports. Whenever a passing motorist honked or gave him a thumbs up, Burl congratulated himself on a job well done. Still, he knew that his billboard mostly reaffirmed the sentiments of folks who already agreed with him. In order to extend his reach, he was looking into renting billboards in the liberal enclaves of the cities — Columbus, Indianapolis, Cincinnati — even Louisville was getting a little pink around the edges. City folks needed a wake-up call. Their problem was that they devoured a steady diet of left-wing propaganda coming from mainstream media, rather than consuming the raw facts, like those from Burl's favorite sources, including Fox News, Breitbart, and Infowars.

Burl watched as one of those dwarfish, so-called "smart" cars, which looked like a rolling suppository, rounded the bend, hit the brakes, and pulled over to the side of the road in front of the billboard. On its rear bumper was a sticker that read Coexist, with each of the letters fashioned out of some world religious symbol, and its rear window was tinted with a rainbow flag. The driver and passenger—a woman and man "of color," as it was politically correct to say—got out of the car. They stood there looking at the billboard long enough that Burl surmised they must be giving it serious thought. Good! Maybe a light bulb of truth was clicking on in their heads.

After a few more seconds, they got back into the car and drove off.

"Does this look okay now, Mr. Slocum?"

"It's practically a work of art, kid. C'mon down."

Justin scrambled down the ladder and hopped off three rungs from the bottom. He wobbled when he landed but righted himself and clicked his heels as if he'd meant to do that.

"Careful, kid. If you break your neck, it's your own damn fault for being stupid."

"Don't worry about me, Mr. Slocum. I'm indestructible."

"Yeah, I was too when I was young."

Burl stretched to retrieve the wallet from the back pocket of his overalls. *Damnation,* he thought. *If I get any fatter, I won't be able to reach around myself.*

He removed two twenty-dollar bills. Justin held out his hand.

"So, I owe you for twenty hours of work, and that comes to two hundred bucks. This $40 is for you to keep. And this...." he opened a lunch box by his feet and took out a small sealed envelope, "is worth $160. Mind, now, that it's for your pappy. I don't want to hear you've pinched any of the product."

"No, sir," Justin said, taking the money and the envelope. "My pappy said I should tell you thanks and that I can work as much as you need me to."

Burl patted Justin on his shoulder. "You're welcome, kid. Tell your pappy that I thank him for his service."

"Yessir. So, then, I'll be back to finish painting the barn Thursday after school."

Before Justin could get away, Burl asked, "By the way, do you ever hear from your Aunt Mazie? What's she up to these days?"

"I don't hear much of nothin' 'bout her ever since she left for Columbus."

"You're OK, kid," Burl told Justin.

He meant it. Most teenagers just didn't have any drive or work ethic anymore. As an entrepreneur, Burl found it encouraging to find a young man who was willing, even eager, to put in an honest day's work for a fair day's pay, instead of begging, thieving, or—worse—going on the government dole.

"Now get on home. Your pappy is waiting for you."

No direct route connected Golden Springs to Coon Creek. To get from one to the other, you had to drive around the nature preserve and cross the river on a steel bridge south of the Clifton Gorge. While Meredith drove, she pointed out landmarks and points of interest along the way, although Roscoe seemed only to care about how long it was taking to get there. Since he wasn't listening to her, she turned on the radio to NPR. Terry Gross was interviewing a grand wizard of the Ku Klux Klan.

Meredith said, "It makes my blood boil to hear such racist bullshit," expecting that Roscoe would have something contemptuous to say. Instead, she heard snoring. He had nodded off.

The Hungry Coon Diner was at the only stoplight in town. Meredith parked in a far corner of the lot, away from the motorcycles, pickup trucks, and assorted candidates for the junkyard that occupied spaces nearer the entrance. The door squeaked as if in pain when they entered. Meredith positioned herself between Roscoe and the seating area so he would not see the turning heads, and led him to the case where the pies were displayed. Roscoe placed both hands on the top of the case and sniffed in deep spurts, as if chewing with his nose.

"What can I get yah for?" the woman behind the counter asked. Her name tag read "Howdy, my name is Edith."

Roscoe asked, "Are you the pie maker?"

"Sure as shootin' I am. And I got blue ribbons from the county fair to prove it." Edith pointed at the regally decorated wall behind her. "What can I get yah for?"

Unable to settle upon any single pie, Roscoe bought four to take home: a dutch apple pie with a lattice top, fresh out of the oven; a rhubarb pie, because he'd never had one before; a key lime pie, because it reminded him of summer; and of course a pecan pie, because in his informed opinion there was no finer dessert made in America.

Meredith was relieved when they left the café. She could ignore the stares, but worried that Roscoe might blow his top if he saw them. They each carried two boxed pies, which fit tight in the space beneath her car's hatchback. When she walked around to the driver's side, Roscoe took a step back, onto the sidewalk.

"I feel like taking a walk," he said.

Oh shit, Meredith thought. "Sure," she said.

Meredith was reluctant to spend any more time than necessary in Coon Creek. Traversing the downtown area gave her the heebie-jeebies. It wasn't just that people stopped in their tracks to look at her, but they held their gaze, as if they'd never seen a black woman before. On the surface, most were polite. Folks passing by wished her good afternoon, or sometimes even attempted superficial small talk, but their conviviality seemed contrived. She imagined them sticking out their tongues as soon as she turned her back.

The feeling was nothing like walking the streets of Golden Springs. There, the citizens and shopkeepers had welcomed her with such ardor that it made her feel self-conscious. When she'd started at Antaeus College, she couldn't so much as go to the grocery store without somebody accosting her to proclaim how much they cherished inclusion and thanked her for making Golden Springs a more diverse community. It made her feel as if she checked off some imaginary box labeled "black lesbian." Vanessa had warned her she might feel that way, so, of course, she had to deny it when they talked on the phone.

Downtown Cook Creek encompassed both sides of Main Street for five blocks, up one side and down the other. Roscoe and Meredith started walking at the town square, which had a small park, a gazebo, a couple of benches, a fountain that never worked, and the statue of the town's founding father, Philander Fink. From there, they walked past the Drink Here Tavern, the Sleeping In mattress shop, a Goodwill store, 7-Eleven, the Fair Deal pawn shop, the Second Chance used-tire store, the Stay in Your Lane bowling alley, the Cut Above barbershop, Henshaw's IGA grocery story, a US Army recruiting office, a nonspecific repairs shop, and several shuttered storefronts.

Roscoe paused to tear down a flyer stapled to a telephone pole. He read aloud from it: "Come one and all. Patriotic Fourth of July fireworks Boom-a-Thon, Coon Creek High School stadium, sponsored by the city of Coon Creek and Life Eternal Funeral Services." He then observed, "Sounds pretty white to me."

"That's safe to say," Meredith confirmed.

Meredith and Roscoe crossed the street and walked back in the direction from whence they'd come. They passed Joe's Sunoco, where four men stood looking under the hood of a Subaru, baffled. They paused to allow a pale woman pushing a double stroller with two fussy infants to cross in front of them and enter the Dream On beauty salon.

"Are there any brothers or sisters in this town?" Roscoe asked.

"Not many," Meredith replied. "But, once I was here on a Sunday morning, and I heard some soul singing at the Hallelujah Church of God in Christ."

They continued. Two teenagers standing in a narrow niche between a drug store and a vacant florist shop vaped huge cumulus clouds of sweet-smelling smoke. Roscoe sneezed in their direction. A tattered flag flew in front of the US Post Office. A man wearing a Chief Wahoo baseball cap sat in a parked car and drank from a brown paper bag. Roscoe looked in the window of Boog's Tattoo Parlor, where a burly man wearing dog tags was sitting in the client's chair, reading *Guns 'n'*

Ammo magazine, with a sidearm pistol strapped to his hip. Roscoe stopped and stared; the man looked up from his magazine and stared back. Meredith, who'd kept walking, doubled back to fetch Roscoe and diverted his attention by saying, "Look at that."

Roscoe's eyes ping-ponged back and forth. "Look at what?" he asked.

Meredith pointed at the nearest storefront, which was the campaign headquarters for "Reverend Belvedere for mayor: have faith in government, for a change."

"Outrageous," Roscoe declared. "Whatever happened to the separation of church and state? Only atheists are fit for political office."

At length they completed their circuit of Coon Creek's core by returning to the town square. There, Roscoe stepped in front of the life-sized bronze statue of Philander Fink and stared it in the eye. Fink had his knees slightly bent but his back straight, held a musket in one hand, and had the other shielding his brow, as if gazing toward the horizon. He wore a coonskin cap, which was home to a nest of starlings. Bird droppings splattered his shoulders.

"Who is this fool?"

Meredith had never really paid any attention to the statue. She read from a plaque embedded in a stone behind it:

> *Philander Fink, 1772–1812, an early explorer of the untamed lands north of the Ohio River, built a cabin at the confluence of Coon Creek and the Little Miami River. This monument is dedicated to him and the spirit of discovery that his memory still inspires in the citizens of Coon Creek.*

"Revisionist history," Roscoe said. "Such deplorables."

Meredith wondered what he meant by that but wasn't about to ask. "Are you ready to drive back to Golden Springs?" she asked.

"Let's get out of this place," he said. "I don't want to be here after dark."

CHAPTER 4

Mazie told herself that she wasn't embarrassed to be white trash from Coon Creek, per se. She just didn't want anybody to know. It was kind of like having done time in prison. Given a choice, she preferred not to mention it.

She honestly loved lots of things about her hometown—her family, of course, even though her brother had shit-for-brains; her seventh grade English teacher, Ms. Nixon, who'd encouraged Mazie to become a writer, mostly because her grades in all subjects other than English were solid Cs; summer bluegrass concerts at the gazebo in the town square, where she used to listen and sit with her feet in the fountain, until they canceled the concerts and turned off the fountain; the Fourth of July Boom-a-Thon at the high school stadium, where every year people swore the fireworks show was better than the last one, even if it wasn't; Edith Doody's homemade pies at the Hungry Coon Diner, of course—and she was sure she could come up with other stuff, too, if she really sat down and thought about it. She loved her hometown for those things, sure. But they weren't nearly enough, so she got the hell out of there as soon as she turned eighteen. If somebody asked her, point blank, if she was from Coon Creek, she wouldn't deny it. But when they asked where she was from, she said Columbus.

Mazie felt that to succeed in the summer program, she needed to embellish her personal history, just a bit, lest Professor Alolo or her fellow students get the idea that she was nothing more than an unwashed hillbilly. So, when the professor asked the class to write their autobiographies, Mazie took poetic license with certain facts. Instead of attending kindergarten through high school in Coon Creek, Mazie wrote that she was born and educated in the upscale suburb New Albany, where she attended the Columbus Academy and entered the gifted students writing program (well, she *had* once participated in a spelling bee there). She came upon her social consciousness by virtue of being the daughter of a labor attorney (her father was a union steward—close enough) and a successful businesswoman (her mother certainly always had some kind of get-rich-quick scheme) who advocated for women's rights in the workplace. Upon graduation, she was accepted at Yale and Dartmouth, but turned them down to attend Oberlin College, which had a mission more focused on her progressive egalitarian values (she had really applied there, as well as Otterbein and Denison, but got denied at all; instead, she went to community college and then Ohio State). Upon graduating with a dual major—English (true) and political science (not exactly, although she had taken a couple of courses)—she went to work as a freelance writer (sort of true; she had published a couple of thousand-word pieces in *Columbus Underground*, for which she was not paid). Soon she would start graduate school (in the form of free online classes). Ultimately, she wanted to establish her own peer-reviewed journal of experimental poetry and fiction by and for women (true) and nonbinary persons (well, why not?).

When Mazie was satisfied with her story, she turned it in to Professor Alolo by sliding it under the door to his office. She was pleased to have finished the assignment, but also worried, because if he bothered to fact check it, she was toast.

It wasn't easy keeping her alter egos straight in her mind. She'd been lying to people other than just Professor Alolo. So far as her parents knew, she worked as an investigative journalist for a major internet-news organization. She covered her tracks by saying that her job required her to travel a great deal, so she was gone often, and much too busy to visit home, even for a weekend. Maybe she could get away at Thanksgiving. Maybe.

Mazie lied to her family for their own good. Her parents would not approve of her participating in any kind of a boondoggle that involved Antaeus College. They, like most folks in Coon Creek, mocked Antaeus as a haven for rich hippies' kids, where they could get academic credit just for being weird. At Antaeus, absent-minded professors expounded from their ivory towers about the glories of feminism, liberalism, socialism, and environmentalism, while denouncing the evils of sexism, capitalism, conservatism, and this-ism or that-ism, depending on their cause of the day. Everybody at Antaeus was high all the time. Nobody there had ever worked a day in their lives, and they looked down at people who did. In the eyes of many citizens of Coon Creek, having a child attend Antaeus College would have made her family pariahs.

When Mazie left for college, her mother told her she was proud of her, but also cautioned her not to "get too big for your britches." At first, Mazie thought that meant not to get fat, but in time she realized that it was a warning not to get snooty and think she was better than her roots. Wasn't that the whole point, though? The way she saw it, success by Coon Creek standards was failure by hers.

After dropping off her autobiography, Mazie returned to her room, belly flopped onto her bed, and buried her face in the pillow, hiding from her conscience.

Rufus Cobb knew he didn't know what he was doing. He was supposed to be working on a research project for Professor Alolo—to find out everything he could about some local historical figure named "Philander Fink." Research had never been Rufus's strong suit, though. Other than to google the guy's name, he was at somewhat of a loss for what else to do. So, he took his questions to the reference department at the Antaeus College Library, where the librarian seemed grateful to be asked and promised to get back to him soon. *Cool,* Rufus thought, *everything should be so easy.*

As Professor Alolo's assistant, Rufus had a key to his office. He sometimes let himself into the office and sat in the professor's chair, just to see what it felt like. After leaving the library, he had some time on his hands, so he smoked a joint and started thinking about his class assignment. Too bad the reference librarian couldn't do that for him too. He didn't think he could pack enough material into his autobiography to make it to three thousand words. Except for the four years he'd gone to the University of Toledo, he'd lived his whole life just getting by in East Cleveland. His story probably wasn't nearly as interesting as everybody else's. So, unable to get started, Rufus went to the professor's office, imagining he could absorb some of the Alolo mojo to inspire him.

The professor's desk was a mess. Rufus took this as evidence of a tumultuously creative mind, buzzing with so many ideas that Professor Alolo could never put anything away before taking off on some new flight of fancy. Covering the surface were Post-it pads, a pile of paper clips, a box of tissues, overstuffed file folders, books with multiple bookmarks, unlabeled compact discs, doodles on pages ripped from a spiral notebook, pens and pencils, and a pencil holder containing scissors, a letter opener, a tube of superglue, and chopsticks. Also on the desk, centered, was a single autobiography, which someone had turned in early. Alolo had placed it in front of the computer monitor, as if it was next in line for his attention. Rufus could hardly avoid reading it. It was Mazie's.

Her story surprised him. Something about the woman it described and the Mazie that he'd met didn't jibe. Usually, Rufus could pick out a privileged white chick upon a single glance. They were all about air kisses and back rubs; their attitude of entitlement was evident in how they flipped their hair, flashed their nails, walked as if strutting down a fashion runway, and posed every time they entered a room. That just wasn't how Mazie operated; and yet, her story read like it belonged to a bona fide rich bitch. How, he then wondered, could she have qualified for one of the two discretionary scholarships awarded to students who could not otherwise afford to attend. These contradictions made her *more* alluring.

The desk phone rang, making Rufus nearly jump out of his sandals. *Busted!* he immediately thought. When the phone rang again, he scolded himself for being so paranoid. *Take a breath,* he told himself. He picked up the phone and answered, "This is the office of Roscoe Alolo."

A woman's voice quavered on the other end, "Oh, uh." She paused for a breath and then continued, "I'm calling in reference to your stud services."

Wow, Rufus thought. *Professor Alolo's got it going on.* "Huh?" he blurted.

"Oh?" The woman seemed as baffled as he was. "Well, I found this here number listed with the American Boxer Club. I'm trying to get in touch with Mr. Roscoe A-loo-loo."

"Uh huh. That's A-lo-lo." At that moment, Rufus gazed out the window and saw Mazie bending over to latch Shabazz to his leash, and suddenly a lightning bolt of comprehension struck him between the eyes. "Yeah, you called the right number. But he isn't here. I can take a message, though."

"Good. What's your name, young man?"

"My name is Rufus. I'm Mr. Alolo's assistant?"

"Well, you see, Mr. Rufus, I'm plumb new at this dog-breeding business. I have a, well, I guess it's okay to say—a *bitch*—who is ready for puppies. She's an all purebred, certified, registered American boxer. So, you see, I need to find me a stud dog to, well, *service* her. I called some kennels, but they're far away and too expensive on top of that. But then I saw that Mr. A-lo-lo had a local number, so I hope that maybe we can make us some kind of an arrangement."

"Sure. I feel yah." He glanced out the window and saw Mazie digging in her heels, trying to restrain

Shabazz from chasing a squirrel. "He's an excellent dog. I bet he'd spawn some great puppies. So, listen, give me your contact information, and I'll have Professor Alolo give you a call."

"*Professor* Alolo?"

"That's right. He's a professor of literature here at Antaeus College. Maybe you've heard of him?"

Rufus heard a man's voice whisper something on the other end; somebody else had been listening to the call. It sounded like he said *fuck me!* There was an unintelligible back and forth between the two of them before the woman shushed her companion and returned to the conversation.

"No. I ain't never heard of him. You see, I don't read very much. But, yeah of course, please have him call me. Tell him to ask for Gertrude."

Rufus mouthed the name *Gertrude* silently. It sounded like something you said when somebody sneezed. The idea that he was talking to somebody named Gertrude suddenly seemed hilarious. It was even funnier when he said it out loud. "Sure, Gertrude. What's your phone number, Gertrude. I'll have him call you, Gertrude. Goodbye, Gertrude."

When he hung up, he convulsed with laughter. *Gertrude! Really?!?*

Toad sat across the counter from Edith Doody, who placed a plate of mixed-berry pie in front of her. She tucked her napkin into her collar and wore it like a bib.

"You want some whupped cream on that?" Edith asked, shaking a cannister of whipped cream in front of Toad's face.

"Well now, Edith, have you ever known me to say no to whipped cream? I could eat a bowl of it, with or without pie."

Chuckling, Edith pressed the nozzle on the cannister and swirled the stream of whipped cream as it squirted out. She layered it row upon narrowing rows, until, with a flourish, she released an extra dollop on the very top.

"That looks almost too pretty to eat," Toad joked, then took a bite. Wearing a whipped-cream mustache, she commented, "A million bucks couldn't buy a better piece of pie."

"Pffft. If I could get a million dollars for a piece of pie, it'd sure solve most of my problems. What the hey, though, I'd be happy with just, say, ten thousands, y' know, enough to fix up my old Bonneville, replace my water heater, get Earl that riding lawn mower he's always wanted, and maybe buy some new shoes."

"We can dream."

"In Coon Creek, even dreaming's too expensive." Edith sighed as deep as if she exhaled a piece of her soul. "But I shouldn't complain. I got it better'n a lot of folks hereabouts. I got my regular customers, ain't that right, Burl?"

Burl Slocum, seated by himself in a booth and eating his lunch of chicken-fried steak and gravy, did not hear, or heard and did not wish to answer.

Toad leaned across the counter and whispered to Edith, "You sure wouldn't know to look at him that he's probably the richest man in town. Whatever he does with his money, he sure don't spend it on clothes."

"Not on tips, neither," Edith said, then, cupping a hand against her mouth, added, "I hear tell that not all of his money is gotten honestly."

"Well, now." Toad had an opinion on that subject but held her tongue. Instead, she changed the subject. "But guess what? It looks like my own little investment is a-gonna pay off real soon."

"Are you talking about that mutt of yours?"

"Dixie ain't no mutt, she's a 100% purebred, certified American boxer, and I found somebody what's got a male boxer to be her stud. If they make puppies, I can sell 'em for $1,000 apiece, maybe more."

"For a dog! Ain't there enough flea-bitten pooches at the animal shelter what anybody can have for free?"

"I agree. But breeders, they pay top dollar for a dog with all the right papers and such. Rich people ain't like you and me. I get a dog for companionship, loyalty. They get dogs to show off. And $1,000 ain't no more to them than a dollar to you or me."

"Who's this high roller whose dog's gonna make puppies with your Dixie dog?"

"He's a professor at Antaeus College."

Out of the blue, Burl Slocum spat out, "Oooh, la de dah, one of them high-and-mighty intellectuals that have nothing better to do than tell a working man how he ought to live."

"Burl Slocum! Shut your mouth!" Toad snapped. "That's the owner of the dog that might be the father of my dog's puppies you're a-besmirching."

"It's true, ain't it," Burl returned. "Them liberals are so full of themselves they think their shit smells like English lavender."

With her back to Burl Slocum, Toad rolled her eyes and stuck out her tongue. Edith winked in agreement.

Toad picked up where she'd left off conversing with Edith. "Next time Daisy goes into heat, I'm to call this professor. He says he'll meet me halfway between here 'n' there, to get the deed done."

"Really? Where?"

"Up at Shawnee Knob. He says it's his dog's favorite place."

"Huh?" Edith asked, then answered herself, "It sounds almost like Tramp inviting Lady to an Italian restaurant for a spaghetti and meatball dinner."

"Well...." It had been years since Toad had seen that movie, so she played the scene in her head. "Now that you mention it, I guess that, in a way, it is sorta romantic."

CHAPTER 5

"The real truth is that, other than old books on my girlfriend's father's bookshelf, I had never heard of Roscoe Alolo."

Behind him, Roscoe boomed, "I trust you've heard of me now, Mr. Nguyen."

All ambient chatter in the room ceased abruptly.

"Begging pardon, sir," Quang said and stood up so he could bow to him. "I meant to say that my girlfriend's father—rest his soul—admired your work."

"Indeed," Professor Alolo said. "It's good to know that the dead remember me fondly."

A gaunt man wearing khakis and a T-shirt with a peace sign entered the room behind him, and together they descended the aisle to the front of the seminar room. The man waved at the class with both hands.

Professor Alolo folded his arms and swept his gaze across the room, making brief but intense eye contact with every one of the "associates"—that's what he called his students. It occurred to him that he was, in fact, old enough to be most of their fathers—well, more likely their *grandfathers*—but he crowded that notion out of his head.

"Good morning," he said. "Before we start, I want to introduce you to Mr. Pat Oglesby. He asked for a moment of our time to say something to you. So, listen."

"Thank you, Doctor Alolo." The man pressed his palms together in a namaste gesture. "My name is *Pax*, not Pat. P-A-X. It is Latin for 'Peace.' Pax Oglesby. I'm the facilitator of the common good in Golden Springs."

"That's like being a mayor," Professor Alolo explained from a seat in the front row, where he chugged a Red Bull while flipping through screens on his cell phone.

Pax Oglesby beamed when he spoke. "On behalf of the people of Golden Springs, Antaeus College, its board of directors, and its faculty, students, and alumni, I welcome you to the 2016 Emerging Writers Summer Literary Arts Residency and Workshop. This is the forty-third year of this program, and I know you will find it as rewarding as many of our past graduates, who have gone to achieve great success. We in Golden Springs are honored to have the eminent Doctor Roscoe Alolo with us as a visiting scholar for one year, and as director of the workshop. For many years, he has been a leading voice in socially-conscious fiction, combining the creative force of a poet's soul and an activist's passion."

Roscoe set aside his cell phone and sat up straighter in his seat.

"On a personal note, I read *Head in Search of a Brain* when I was an undergraduate, and at the time I considered it one of the most visionary books I had ever read."

Roscoe noted the use of past tense.

"But what I wanted to say most of all is that you are now all members of the Golden Springs family. While you are here this summer, I especially want to invite you to be part of our community's Independence Day Festival of Lights. It is a joyous celebration of our values, accomplishments, and dreams for a more free and egalitarian society. Trust me, it is unlike any other Fourth of July you've ever seen, culminating in our totally unique Ascent of the Luminaries. You have to see it to believe it."

"Thank you for your hospitality," Roscoe called out from his seat.

Oglesby bowed. One person applauded, then another, and pretty soon everybody clapped, although with about as much enthusiasm as if they were shooing flies.

As soon as Oglesby left the room, Professor Alolo stood, stepped forward, tapped his cane, and climbed the central aisle in the seminar room, one arduous step at a time. He stopped halfway up and slowly turned his head backwards, catching his breath before speaking. "I see that each of you is sitting in the same seats as you were yesterday." He tsked and shook his head. "Why is that? What compels a free person who can sit anywhere to mindlessly plop themselves down in the same seat, time after time?"

The woman wearing a hijab zipped her backpack, got up, and went to sit in a different seat.

"Change is the engine of art. Good writing is a chronicle of change. It reflects the perspective of a person whose imagination cannot be contained by the status quo. If that doesn't describe you, then you'll never write anything worth a damn.

"This is just the second day of class. It didn't take long for you to disappoint me. A new record! Already, you have gotten stuck in dull habits. Dull, dull, dull. I expect more from you. Are you so afraid of change that you can't even find the courage to sit in a different chair? If so, then why are you here?"

The woman in the hijab spoke up, "I fear nothing."

"Shut up! That was a rhetorical question. I know why you are here. Do you want me to explain it to you?"

That, too, was a rhetorical question. Professor Alolo let the class marinate on it for a few seconds. Their passive anticipation reminded him of what he loved most about being a celebrity — the rapt way that people used to listen to him.

"You are here to learn *how* to change. And do you know what about yourselves you need to change first?"

He leaned forward with both hands on his cane, daring any wiseass to try to answer him.

"It's simple. You are writers in search of purpose. But you can't start a fire with wet matches. You are writers of words. I will show you how to be writers of ideas.

"Let's get started then. You need to generate some synergy amongst yourselves. The truth is I expected you all to sit in the same seat — everybody does, always. So, I taped an envelope beneath each of your chairs. Please look at them now."

At once, the associates bent down or knelt in front of their seats and reached beneath them. The woman in the hijab went back to her original seat for hers. Each person retrieved a plain white envelope. Inside was a 3" x 5" card with a single digit written in black magic marker on it. Some waved their cards as if they were lucky winners at bingo; others looked once at their cards and then placed them face down on their laps, unwilling to divulge their numbers before they knew what was going on. The scene reminded Professor Alolo of folks waiting for their numbers to be called at a busy delicatessen.

"Find the people with the same number as yours. They belong to your group. There will be four groups, each with five persons. I did not assign these numbers arbitrarily. No, based upon your autobiographies, your backgrounds, and your demographics, I put you together to ensure creative tension. I want you to disagree, to argue, to bicker. And then, I want you to work together."

There were so many blank expressions that they seemed to ask, collectively, "Huh?"

"Your next assignment will be a group writing project. I want each group to write a manifesto. Find a purpose that unites you. Sound a call for action. Develop a vision. In words and deeds, in poetry, prose, and narrative, make a statement to change hearts and minds, to right a wrong, promote a cause, render justice. Are there any questions?"

Professor Alolo was encouraged that nobody asked any questions. That meant they were all too confused to admit it. This pleased him; he always counted on other people to figure out what he meant, because he didn't always know himself. That's what critics and students were for. Sometimes they found deep meanings in his work that he'd never noticed.

"So what are you waiting for?" he said and clapped his hands over his head. "Get moving!"

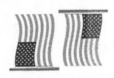

Contrary to Professor Alolo's presumption, Mazie had *not* sat in the same seat; she had sat one row closer to the front than at the first class. So far as she could tell, though, he was right about everybody else. That made her feel kind of proud. She could've reached under the chair behind her to retrieve the envelope, but instead she walked to the end of the row, stepped up, and did a U-turn, making sure that the professor saw her.

Mazie detested group projects; she usually wound up doing all the work, then sharing the credit equally with the freeloaders, or shouldering the blame if it sucked. Even worse, though, was being in a group where everybody had passionate opinions. Passionate people were a pain in the ass. All the inevitable debate, dispute, compromise, and concession wore her down, until she no longer cared anymore. Either way, her heart sank like an anchor when she heard Professor Alolo mention a group project.

"Group writing" seemed like an oxymoron. Mazie much preferred the solitary, introspective process of writing, where she ensconced herself in her private reality: writing by candlelight, sipping wine, listening to Windham Hill music, oblivious to the world around her. Woe to anybody who trespassed upon her ruminations, as her family, her college roommates, and myriad boyfriends had discovered. When she was writing, she wouldn't abide interruptions. Inspiration demanded isolation.

Mazie cupped her hand and looked at her card. Her number was four. Meanwhile, her fellow associates were already mixing among themselves, checking and comparing who had what numbers and organizing themselves accordingly. Mazie sauntered around the groups as they formed, just close enough to eavesdrop. When she found her cohort, she looked around for the nearest exit. If she were waiting for an elevator, and the next car to arrive contained those same four people, she'd have waved them on and waited.

"Yo, yo, yo, Maze. You must be the last number four. C'mon. We're over here," Rufus Cobb called, waving to her as if hailing a cab.

Seated with Rufus in a rear corner of the room were Quang Nguyen; the woman in the hijab, whose name was Taara Ali; and an old leathery man with multiple tattoos, a pony tail, and a braided beard, whom people called El Jefe. Mazie felt their collective gaze wash over her, like she was standing in a one-person police lineup. She squirmed into the nearest vacant seat next to Taara Ali.

"Salaam," Taara said to Mazie.

"Is this the number four team?" Mazie asked. *What a bunch of wack jobs*, she thought.

Quang: "That's us. United by fate."

Rufus: "We're the Team of Strangers."

El Jefe shifted forward in his seat and addressed the group, "So, if I heard right, the professor wants us to write a manifesto, like Marx or Mao or the Unabomber."

Taara Ali jabbed her finger at the air and said, "We write to change people's minds."

"Huh?" Mazie asked.

"I wake up every day wondering what has changed overnight," Quang said. "It makes me feel like a new person every day."

El Jefe: "That sounds more like a fortune cookie than a manifesto."

Taara: "All change returns to the past."

"Huh?" Mazie asked.

"Chillax, people," Rufus piped up. "I know exactly what Professor Alolo looks for. I know how his mind works. For example, at the end of *Head in Search of a Brain*, just before Citizen Z pushes a pie into the face of

Beloved Leader, he yells at him, 'You can ignore me. But you can't ignore this.'"

"Say something that makes sense to me, amigo," El Jefe said.

"The professor wants us to write something that's the equivalent of smearing a pie into somebody's face." Rufus twisted his open palm side to side, smearing an invisible pie into an invisible face.

Taara snapped her fingers and declared, "Protest! Manifestation! Civil disobedience!"

El Jefe: "In America, protest is like sport."

Quang took notes. "Sounds like fun."

Taara: "You must begin by undoing everything that you've done."

El Jefe: "Out with the new, in with the old. Meet the new boss, same as the old boss. The French Revolution led to the Reign of Terror. The Russian Revolution led to Stalinism. The American Revolution led to the War of 1812, which led to the Civil War. World War I led to World War II, which has led to too many new wars to count."

Taara: "So, too, in my country. Always at war. First the British invaded, and we pushed them out. Then came Russia, then Al-Qaeda, mujahideen, Taliban, and now the Americans."

El Jefe: "Dialectical-fucking-materialism."

"Exactamundo," Rufus declared, raising his hand above his head to solicit a high five from El Jefe, who ignored it and continued, "Marx figured all this bullshit out years ago, but history didn't listen to him. To get real change, you've got to turn the past upside down."

Mazie shook her head in confusion. "What's any of this got to do with *writing*?"

The way they looked at her, she might as well be wearing a sign that said Kick Me around her neck. She sought Rufus's eyes, looking for support. But she couldn't discern what he was thinking behind the wry expression on his face. "Oh, never mind," she mumbled.

The group responded:

"No."

"Naw."

"Nuh uh."

"Negative."

"Think about what's happening here, "Rufus said. "Professor Alolo told us that he organized our groups to create diversity. Well, just look at us. I'm from the east side of Cleveland. Quang, you're what — second generation Vietnamese?"

"Yep. My grandparents fled when Hanoi fell. Barely made it out. No thanks to Americans."

"And Taara, you're what — Iranian?"

"No."

"Iraqi?"

"No."

"Syrian?"

"No, no, no. I am Afghani."

"That was my next guess."

"Of course. Americans only know countries where they've been in wars. But I live in Montreal now. You would not believe the disrespect I had to endure just to enter your country."

El Jefe jumped in, "And I was brought here when I was just a baby, in a rubber raft from Cuba. I had no choice."

Mazie put her hands on her hips, like a gunslinger preparing to draw. "And I guess that makes me just a white person," she said.

"No, not just any white person. A white *woman*," Rufus specified.

Mazie wondered what she was doing there, if this was really Ohio—well, geographically it was, although culturally Golden Springs was more of an idea than a place.

"Alright, then, let's get started." Rufus gestured for the others to huddle around him. "Like I said, I know how Professor Alolo thinks. I have an idea. Listen up...."

During their residency, the so-called "associates" lodged in Bard Hall, an undergraduate dormitory haunted by the tipsy ghosts of countless legendary parties. According to local folklore, Bard was the hands-down campus champion for wild parties, rampant sex, and other forms of collegiate debauchery. It seemed to Mazie as if something in the building's ambiance stimulated hormones, because her fellow associates— *adults!*—acted like unsupervised freshmen away from mom and dad for the first time in their lives.

Trying to write amid the bedlam of the dormitory was like trying to perform brain surgery at a monster truck rally. Mazie had a ritual for writing. She needed, first, to do her breathing exercises, to purge the tension from her body and the angst from her mind. Second, she required a cozy, intimate space, surrounded by familiar objects, lots of pillows, and mood enhancers like incense, furry slippers, new age music, fresh flowers, and a glass (or two) of white wine. Dormitory life, though, reminded her of weekends in the trailer park on the outskirts of Coon Creek, where good times invariably led to the cops being called to break up a party, or a fight, or some domestic contretemps — usually all three.

Somebody down the hall shouted, "Vodka Jell-O shots in the common room!"

Mazie dropped her head onto her desk and groaned. Not that she had anything against vodka Jell-O shots in the proper time and place, but it rankled her that she'd come to Antaeus expecting to immerse herself in serious literature within a community of fellow artists, and so far evenings in the dormitory rivalled Saturday nights on High Street, back in her undergraduate years at Ohio State. Mazie was glad that she had finally put those days of booze, sex, and headbanger music behind her. Maybe later, for the sake of being sociable, she'd go have a couple of beers with her dorm mates. In the meantime, though, the nightly hijinks were a damn nuisance. She had *work* to do.

Mazie glanced at the clock; it was already 7:00 p.m., time to take Shabazz for his evening walk. She put on her tennis shoes and left the room. Before she could make a clean getaway, Rufus Cobb came out of the coed washroom, wearing only a towel, and seeing her, stopped in his tracks. Mazie was on course to pass him and had no choice but to keep walking. After listening to his nutty idea in the group earlier that afternoon, though, Rufus was just about the last person she wanted to talk to.

"Yo, yo, yo. Maze. Happy hour is in the other direction," Rufus said and pointed. His towel was dripping and hanging low.

"Can't right now. I've got to walk the professor's dog."

Rufus shrugged and said, "Okay. Peace out."

Mazie felt peculiarly disappointed that he'd given up so easily.

It had been a muggy day. The setting sun looked pinkish and fuzzy through a soup of humidity. The sky directly overhead was the shade of dishwater, with a dense, almost grainy, texture. Summer days in this part of Ohio seldom came into focus. Standing out from the haze, though, the campus was an oasis of fresh colors. Every day, all day long, a phalanx of Hispanic landscapers worked the grounds with mowers, blowers, pruners, trimmers, shovels, rakes, and Weedwackers; by the time they left in the afternoon, the tranquility was mesmerizing. The music of a Vivaldi baroque concerto was playing from an open window somewhere. Barefoot lovers sat on a bench in front of the fountain, holding hands while they made goo-goo eyes at each other. Walking the main path through campus, Mazie felt like a tourist in Oz.

Coming toward her in the opposite direction, Dean Meredith Stokes was talking into a cell phone, which she held flat on her open palm in front of her. "Vanessa, please think about it...."

Mazie slowed down to listen as she passed by.

"Please," Meredith said to the person on the other end of the call, oblivious to being overheard. "I can't go to Philly now. What don't you come here for the holiday weekend? I really need to see you."

Normally, Mazie minded her own business, but the dean was carrying on this conversation in speaker mode, so it seemed fair to listen. She was tempted to back up to snoop some more, and might have, had she not already arrived at the alumni house. Shabazz heard her or smelled her coming, because he began barking deliriously before she reached the porch.

Mazie opened the door and called inside, "Hello. Professor. It's me."

Shabazz greeted her by jamming his head into her groin and snorting; a gesture of affection, she supposed, though it bothered her a bit that the dog sniffed her crotch so vigorously, as if smelling something very enticing to him.

"C'mon, boy. Let's go," she said and fastened his leash to his collar.

From the parlor, behind a closed door, Roscoe Alolo called, "Mazie? Is that you? Please come here."

Mazie winced. Shabazz scratched the door to be let out. "Just a minute, buddy," Mazie said to the dog.

The parlor door groaned when Mazie pushed it. Professor Alolo made her nervous; he was a genius, after all. At least, that's what she'd read about him. She found the "genius" wearing a T-shirt and boxer shorts, seated in an antique fauteuil chair with his feet on an ottoman, hot water bottles on both knees, and a nearly-empty bottle of Jamaican rum on the end table next to him.

"Would you care for a sip of Bacardi?" the professor asked.

"I'll pass on that, sir." Mazie somehow felt like she needed to justify her abstinence. "Shabazz is a handful, so I need to be able to keep up with him."

"That's true," Professor Alolo said. "You do a good job controlling him. What's your cell phone number?"

"My number?"

"So that I can contact you in the case of an emergency."

"What kind of emergency?"

"Not so much an emergency, really. More like a window of opportunity. Someday soon I'll need for you to help me, possibly with no advance notice. Shabazz is a stud."

"A what?"

"A stud of great value."

Mazie felt off balance—this sounded weird. "Huh?"

"He is a 100% purebred American boxer in search of a female purebred, and I found one for him. The next time this bitch goes into heat, we need to hurry to bring Shabazz to her so they can mate. I'll need your help. Like you say, he can be a handful."

Shabazz was hard to handle under normal circumstances, but in the presence of a bitch in heat, he might turn into a one-dog stampede.

"What do I have to do?" Mazie asked.

"Control Shabazz. Help me. We will need to hike a bit to reach the rendezvous point that we agreed on."

"Where?"

"At Shawnee Knob. Shabazz likes it there. I suggested it as a compromise, since it's against some campus rule to do it here, and I absolutely refuse to ever set foot again in that other place, where the bitch's owner lives."

Mazie felt her cheeks go numb. "Where is that?"

"*Coon Creek.*" Professor Alolo sneered. "It is a sad, depressed little redneck town. Normally, as you know, I sympathize with the plight of displaced workers. But this place is willfully stuck in the past. Even the name—*Coon Creek*—is offensive. What's that all about?"

"I think it's about raccoons," Mazie answered.

"Never mind. The very first thing you see when you enter that town is a statue of a truly despicable man, a slave catcher no less. But the people of that town revere him as their founding father. I refuse to go back there as long as that statue stands, not even for pie."

Mazie stopped herself from asking what he meant about pie. Professor Alolo asked a second time for her cell phone number. She was so disoriented that she had to look it up, and then after she gave it to him, she immediately wished she'd given him a fake number, with a couple of digits transposed to make it look like an honest mistake. More than anything, she just wanted to get out of there.

"Be sure to leave your phone on at all times," Professor Alolo said to her as she left.

That night, it was Shabazz who had trouble keeping up with Mazie. Every time he halted to raise his leg, she yanked on his leash. At one point he squatted to defecate, but Mazie kept walking straight ahead, so the poor dog had to shit in mid stride.

"Sorry," Mazie said when she realized what she'd done. She scolded herself. It wasn't the dog's fault. Even so, his good fortune created a problem for her.

Why did it have to be Coon Creek? Whoever the other dog's owner was—it could be anybody, since everybody in Coon Creek owned a dog—would certainly recognize her. This could wreck her whole summer. On one hand, if her family found out that she was so close by and what she was doing, they'd be hurt, shocked, angry, disappointed, maybe even hostile. On the other hand, Professor Alolo clearly detested Coon Creek and everything it stood for... which meant her, too? If her cover was blown, Mazie would be unwelcome in either locale.

Mazie bent down to look Shabazz in the eye. "What am I going to do?" she asked him.

Shabazz licked her face.

They walked across the campus, all the way to the Welcome to Golden Springs sign at the city limits, then turned back and kept walking until it was dark. After returning Shabazz to the alumni house, Mazie sat on a nearby bench and watched the clock tower for a while before she finally decided to return to the dormitory. Now, getting drunk seemed like a good idea, even with a bunch of goofball writers. She anticipated that the dorm party would still be going strong.

When Mazie entered the common room, though, nobody was there. The only movement in the whole room was a jiggling bowl full of vodka Jell-O shots. Mazie walked up and down the halls, calling, "Hello, is anybody here?"

A door at the end of the hall opened. One of her classmates rolled out on his wheelchair and said to her, "A bunch of them left a while ago. They said something about civil disobedience. That's all I know, sorry."

"Fuck me," Mazie said to herself. "When I want to be left alone, they're all over me. But when I want some company, they're all gone."

Mazie took the bowl of Jell-O shots back to her room. There, she lay on the bed and began slurping them down, one at a time, in rapid succession. She hoped that if she got drunk enough, she might figure out what to do about her dilemma. Sober, she sure couldn't see any solutions.

CHAPTER 6

Faye Pfeiffer played taps in her mind. She saluted in silent reverence as the last sliver of sun dropped below the horizon, and then she commenced lowering the flag. As soon as she could reach it, she unlatched the clip connecting the bottom of the flag to the line and snapped it into one of her belt loops, then continued lowering the flag until she could undo the upper clip. She held Old Glory in front of her, with her right arm fully extended perpendicular to the ground, as if she were a human flagpole. Over the years, Faye had mastered a technique by which she could perform the normally two-person job of folding the flag according to military standards. It was a modified version of the method she used for folding coffin blankets, although trickier, because she had to hold one end perfectly taut while tucking in the corners one at a time. It was an ungainly procedure, but since she lacked a partner to assist her, it was necessary.

Having folded the flag to perfect specifications, she placed it into a zipped canvas bag and set it on top of her parents' monument, then she too hopped up there and sat with her legs dangling, the toes of her oxfords barely touching the ground. Fireflies appeared in the gloaming; they surrounded Faye in all directions, across the open terrain of the cemetery. Ever since she was a little girl, Faye had spent countless enchanted hours watching the courtship signals of fireflies, how the multitudes of them formed kaleidoscopic patterns of streaks, curlicues, and streams of coordinated movement. She admired their artistry and, even though she knew the notion was silly, she indulged herself to imagine that they had whatever passed as fun for fireflies. She sometimes stayed watching until the last lonely firefly blinked out at the end of another long night's performance. Faye had always wanted to put it to music — Pink Floyd, maybe.

Faye had spent most of that day preparing for the Boom-a-Thon. Working in her embalming lab, she'd compounded a new formula that she hoped would enhance the luster and colors of her fireworks. She was especially anxious to see how the blues turned out; they were the hardest to get right. Additionally, she'd hand-packed shells with an array of stars designed to affect a chain of after-explosions, more spectacular than anything the good citizens of Coon Creek had ever seen. Every year, Faye took pride in manufacturing a Boom-a-Thon fireworks show that was better than the last. Other than the Fourth of July, or when somebody died, she remained pretty much invisible in Coon Creek, so this was the highlight of her social calendar.

Sponsoring Coon Creek's annual Fourth of July Boom-a-Thon extravaganza had been a patriotic tradition of the Life Eternal Funeral Home since the 1960s. Her grandfather, Frederick Pfeiffer, who'd been excused from military conscription due to chronic inflammatory bowel disease, considered it the least he could do to defend life, liberty, and American values. Besides, it made good business sense for the local mortuary services to subsidize such a popular, life-affirming celebration; it helped to offset negative impressions. Even though Frederick died when Faye was a child, everybody who knew him said he was a jovial man with a hearty laugh that often shook the rafters of the Drink Here Tavern, where he reportedly spent a lot of time.

Frederick passed custodianship of the Boom-a-Thon to his son, Wilbur, Faye's father. Wilbur turned eighteen soon after the Vietnam War and the draft ended, so he too never served in the military. Instead, he did his part to serve America by improving and expanding the Boom-a-Thon. Wilbur also started the practice of placing little plastic American flags on the graves of every veteran resting in the Amity Valley Memorial Gardens on Memorial Day. And on Thanksgiving, he took out a full-page ad in the *Coon Creek Picayune* weekly newspaper, thanking veterans for their service.

Wilbur taught his daughter and only child, Faye, the fine art of mixing, packing, staging, and detonating fireworks before she was old enough to drive. Even as a girl, she understood that her father was grooming her to assume not only the family business, but also its annual contribution to the Boom-a-Thon. Still, if she'd only had the chance, after high school she would have enlisted for a stint in the army, especially after they relaxed the rules permitting women to serve in combat operations. She thought she'd be good at it. As she knew all too well, though, death doesn't accommodate one's plans, and when her parents died in a tragic automobile accident, theirs was the first funeral that she conducted all by herself. Duty bade no less of her.

Faye sometimes worried that she had no child of her own to whom she could pass on the family's traditions. True, she figured she still had time for a family. But among the eligible bachelors in Coon Creek, there was nary a one that didn't turn her stomach, let alone whose seed she would willingly bear. Artificial insemination seemed downright romantic by comparison.

In full darkness around eleven, Faye hiked through a grove of tall oaks and maples to the southeastern meadow, a low-lying section of the cemetery where heavy spring rains pooled and frogs croaked so loud it battered her eardrums. Earlier that day, she'd set up her fireworks apparatus there. From this remote spot, she could test her fireworks and they would not be visible from most of the residential blocks in Coon Creek. The only people likely still awake were holed up in the Drink Here Tavern, and even if they saw something, they might not remember it anyway. Faye was confident that she could sneak in a single volley and nobody would notice.

By the light of a lamp strapped to her forehead, Faye mounted three tubes onto the firing board, dropped a shell into each, clipped igniters onto the fuses, and attached wires to the firing system. Counting off steps, she pivoted to face the launching pad, knelt onto one knee, and steadied the detonator on her raised foreleg. She counted backwards from ten, then turned the ignition key.

The explosive flowering of fireworks never failed to take her breath away. Successive, overlapping bursts filled the sky from end to end. The night sky was her canvas. The brilliant colors swirled like a van Gogh starry night, except this was *her* masterpiece. Faye flushed with the thrill of it all. She opened her eyes wide and did not blink, allowing the lights and colors to cascade straight into her cerebral cortex. It felt like an optical orgasm, or at least inasmuch as she imagined what an orgasm felt like.

The Drink Here Tavern wasn't just a place; it was a statement. (You.) Drink. Here. Every person who entered knew exactly what to do. That's what Boog loved about it. Drinking with Tank, Buzz, Red, and Paddy — AKA "the Galoots" — listening to the same classic country music, and talking the same shit about work, weather, sports, women, and politics was akin to a ritual of renewal. It lifted him in good times and reassured him in bad. His favorite way to pass any evening was to plop down onto his designated stool at the end of the bar around dinnertime and shoot the shit with his friends, not moving except to piss or sometimes play pool, until closing time.

It didn't always work out that way, though. All it took was one thing to go awry — like a stranger who looked at him the wrong way or a drunk chick who spurned his advances — to ruin the whole night. On those occasions, he brawled, blacked out, broke something, was asked to leave, or all the above. He didn't take it personally, though. Sometimes messiness was inevitable — shit happens, right?

And Boog knew a thing or two about messy business. That was how he answered anybody who asked him what he did during his tours of duty in Afghanistan—"messy business, really fuckin' messy." And when he said that, he snorted and spat to show how the mere mention of that subject pissed him off, so folks learned real quick not to bring it up again. Not only did he not *want* to talk about it, he insisted that he didn't *need* to talk about it. No counseling or support groups for him, not even a service animal. PTSD was for whiners. Hanging out at the Drink Here Tavern worked a whole lot better than any amount of therapy.

Boog had almost finished his second pitcher of Pabst Blue Ribbon while waiting for the Galoots to show up. He needed to get a head start on them, because none could keep up with his pace of drinking. It was like his handicap. Boog drank straight out of the pitcher, pouring it down his throat from the spout. That way if somebody—usually, his ex-wife—asked him how much he'd had to drink, he could say truthfully "just a couple of beers."

For the most part, the beer was just a decoy, anyway. What really got him buzzing was the oxycodone. He was mostly sure that nobody suspected he popped pills, because he drank enough to explain any stupid shit he did under the influence. It worked like a charm, and nobody was wiser. In Coon Creek's social order, a raging alcoholic was better than an occasional opiate user.

A Cincinnati Reds game was on the bar television, with the sound off and closed-captioning on. Before he went to Afghanistan, the Reds were pretty good. But now, they were embarrassingly awful, even with Joey Votto. It sometimes seemed like everything had fallen apart while he was gone, almost as if Coon Creek couldn't function without him.

Boog belched so loud that something popped in his head. Suddenly, he felt stone-cold sober. That happened sometimes, a reality flashback. Maintaining a steady buzz required constant replenishment. Time for a little vitamin oxy booster. Leaving his baseball cap on the stool to save his seat, Boog stumbled to the men's room.

There were two stalls in the men's room—one had greenish diarrhea slopped all over the toilet seat, and the other had a puddle of rancid liquid on the floor. Boog selected the one with the puddle, because he needed to sit. Once inside, he removed a small Ziploc baggie containing crushed 30-milligram oxycodone pills from his sock, then shook a small portion onto the back of a credit card on his lap. It looked like a little landing strip of sugar. Boog had recently graduated from swallowing whole tablets to crushing and snorting them up his nose, which gave him a faster, more-potent head rush. But he drew the line at injections; that was only for addicts. Boog used oxy for purely recreational purposes, which he deserved considering all the shit and drama that he had to put up with. He especially appreciated how it gave him enough of a second wind to keep drinking until the bar closed, then afterwards he'd pass out and sleep like a baby. Since returning home from that godforsaken hellhole where he spent the worst four years of his life, oxy was just about the only thing that made him feel like himself.

And so long as he got a discount in exchange for his son's work, the costs were, well, sometimes hard to sustain, but generally manageable.

Snorting through a soda straw, Boog felt an electrified sensation in all directions from his sinuses and into his head, then it hit him like lightning when it reached the pleasure center in his brain. He no longer sat on a lopsided toilet seat in a dive bar, but was in a pinball machine, bouncing off bumpers of blinding luminescence, slingshotting across brilliant regions of flashes and sparkles, and exploding in a shower of colors every time he hit a target. He had no thoughts, no memories, no anger or frustrations, just absolute, transcendent bliss. Better than sex, and a lot easier to obtain. It was a preview of heaven. It was all that mattered to Boog anymore.

Boog didn't breathe; it felt like he didn't have to, like the drug provided all the oxygen he needed. After holding his breath for several seconds — not that he counted — he felt a blackout coming on, and, on the verge of passing out, he sucked in a desperate mouthful of air. The equal and opposite reflex was that he vomited profusely onto his lap.

"Ooooh," he groaned. "Aaaah."

He licked his lips. He was now ready to drink some more beer.

Boog cleaned himself with the last of the toilet paper in the stall, then flushed away all evidence of his mishap. Leaving the men's room, he put his hand against the wall to steady himself and waddled forward. He paused at the end of the hallway to map out a path to his bar stool. The song playing over the speakers, "Flushed from the Bathroom of Your Heart" by Johnny Cash, sounded to Boog like the most beautiful song ever written. Every word spoke truth to him. He turned his entire will over to just listening.

Between Boog and the speakers, though, a nasty clamor, which sounded like the braying of coyotes, came from a nearby booth. It ruined the perfection of his moment. Still holding onto the wall, he turned to see where all that caterwauling was coming from.

A group of rank strangers occupied the booth. Not only had Boog never seen them before, but they were also strange, as in just plain fucking weird. They stood out amid the usual crowd at the Drink Here like clowns at a funeral. Among the group was a jive black dude with hair turds bundled on top of his head, like tentacles. There was a caramel brown woman with sunken eyes wearing a layered head rag the likes of which Boog hadn't seen this side of Kandahar. A skinny Asian kid who looked thirteen years old sported a shit-eating grin while doodling on a napkin. The loudest, though, was an old bandito with rings on every finger and frizzy gray hair nearly down to his ass. Even though Boog couldn't make out a word they said, he could tell just by the looks of them that they were talking trash. It made his ribs rattle.

"Ya'll ain't from around here, are ya," Boog shouted at them with no inflection, more a statement than a question.

The group kept right on chattering, either oblivious to Boog or ignoring him. They had to be from Golden Springs because they looked like nothing found anywhere else thereabouts. Every once in a while, some lost souls from Golden Springs drifted into the Drink Here, but usually they stayed only until they found out they couldn't get wine coolers or that, no, the bartender would not turn off the game. If they failed to take the hint, well, Boog felt entitled to defend his territory.

What Boog hated most about them, apart from looking like carnival freaks, was their attitude, as if they were better than everybody else in the room. It took a hell of a lot of moxie to trespass into a working-class bar and look down at the regulars as if they were all no better than yokels, rednecks, and hillbillies. There weren't many places left where a grunt like Boog could have a beer and tell a story among like-minded folks. Venturing outside of Coon Creek to any of the cities—Columbus, Cincinnati, even Dayton for cryin' out loud—felt like visiting another planet. It was as if those people breathed different air. They sure as shit didn't have any business breathing his.

"*I said* where'n the fuck are ya'll from?" Boog repeated, amplifying.

They had to have heard him that time, even though they continued ignoring him, which was the same as saying to him *fuck you, redneck*. He didn't move. He didn't say anything. He just stared at them with simmering malice.

The woman was the first to notice. She leaned forward and whispered something to the others. Finally, the one with the hair turds turned to him and said, "Hey, dude. What's the deal?"

Boog heard that as *hey asshole, you want to take this outside?* His jaws tensed; he balled his hands into fists. There was only one way to answer their impudence. He took one long step in their direction, and then he felt a heavy hand clamp onto his shoulder blade.

"Whoa there, cowboy. Do you want to spend the night in jail?" Burl Slocum asked him.

"Fuck me, Burl. How long can a man be expected to put up with all of this bullshit?"

Burl patted his back. "Don't retaliate like that. If you do, you're just asking for trouble. But if you really want to make them shit their pants, all you've got to do is put your hat back on." He picked up the baseball cap that Boog had left to save his seat at the bar and handed it to him. It was red, with the white embroidered words Make America Great Again.

"Wear it proudly," Burl said.

Boog put the hat on his head, lowered over his brow, and smirked at the outsiders. They quickly huddled up and whispered among themselves. When the group broke from their conference, they hastily finished their drinks, got up, and, without looking at Boog, scampered out of the bar like kids afraid of getting in trouble with their parents.

Boog was elated. It was as if that hat gave him a superpower. From that moment, he resolved never to leave home without it on his head.

Dixie stuck her nose under the sheet and pressed it against the small of Toad's back. Toad snapped awake with her eyes popping out of their sockets and heart hammering so hard she felt her pulse all the way down to her toes. The bedroom was still dark. Zeke kept snoring. Dixie whimpered, walked to the door, and barked again. Toad turned to look at the digital clock, then said out loud, "Four thirty, Dixie. It's too early to go for a walk."

Dixie whimpered and circled her tail nervously.

"Well, well, oh well." Toad swung her feet onto the floor. "I guess when you gotta go, you gotta go."

Toad pulled on a pair of sweatpants over her pajama bottoms, slipped one of Zeke's T-shirts over her head, and worked her feet into a pair of flip-flops without bending over. Dixie led her to the front door, and as soon as Toad opened it enough for her to wiggle through, she dashed into the yard and squatted above a garden gnome, letting go of a long piss.

"I should've known you wouldn't bother me unless it was a real emergency," Toad apologized to the dog.

As soon as she was done, Dixie scampered to the end of the driveway and looked back at Toad with pleading eyes.

"Let's go, then. It ain't like I could fall back to sleep, anyhow."

Attaching the leash to Dixie's collar, Toad took a few steps in the direction of their customary morning walk. Dixie resisted. Toad gave the dog some slack in her leash, and Dixie started pulling like an ox plowing a field toward the opposite end of the block. She seemed to know where she wanted to go. It was all Toad could do to hold on.

"Slow down, girl. What's the matter?"

At the end of the block, Dixie dragged Toad through the alley that led to Main Street, turned the corner, and starting barking at something in the distance. Toad's night vision wasn't what it used to be, but by streetlight she saw a tangle of shadows flutter and take flight on the far side of the town square. They hurried into a car with its lights off and slammed the doors shut so hard they echoed. The vehicle peeled out as it drove into the dark.

"What in the...?"

Dixie gave chase, barking repeatedly, triggering a chain reaction among all the other dogs that heard her. Holding tight to her leash, Toad broke stride and soon ran faster than she had in years. Lights turned on in the trailer park off the alley behind the IGA store. Toad didn't know why, exactly, but something compelled her to call out, "Help!"

The woman and the dog came to a stop, both panting heavily, at the base of the statue of Philander Fink. Toad bent over, hands on her knees, until she caught her breath. When she stood up, she wasn't sure if she saw what she thought she saw. She squinted and stepped onto the curb to get a better view under the streetlight. Dixie rubbed against her side.

The statue of Philander Fink was dressed in a polka-dot dress and wore a straw hat with a price tag dangling from the brim. Hanging from a chain around its neck was a stenciled sign that read, "Take this racist statue down!"

Toad sat on the nearest bench and petted Dixie behind her ears. "What are we going to do about this?" she asked the dog.

CHAPTER 7

Zeke refused to drive because his gout was acting up and he couldn't work the pedals, but Toad suspected the real reason was that he didn't trust his bladder driving on that bumpy road to Shawnee Knob. He would never say so, but she washed his dirty underwear, and she knew that he'd started to leak. Since Zeke was out of commission, Toad asked Boog to drive her to Dixie's big doggie date. When he picked her up, his eyes were kind of glassy. Before she got in the car, Toad sidled close enough to sniff his breath; he smelled like mouthwash.

"I hope you ain't been a-drinking," she said.

"I'm 90% sober," Boog answered.

At least he was being honest. Toad figured that his 90% was better than Zeke's 100%, so she reckoned it was safe to ride with him.

"Let's get a-going, then," she said.

They were already on their way before Toad realized that Justin had stowed away in the back of the pickup.

Toad hadn't been to Shawnee Knob in several years. The spot was home to many cherished memories. When she and Zeke were courting, they often snuck up there after dark to fool around. They might even have conceived Boog there under a harvest moon. Later, when Boog and Mazie were kids, the whole family sometimes piled into the Blazer and drove up there for Sunday afternoon picnics. Boog used to lean over the edge of the cliff and holler down into the valley "diarrhea," then he'd laugh and laugh when the echo answered him back. Mazie would pick purple coneflowers and tie their stems into a headband, which she'd wear all week long. Zeke drank beer and smoked his pipe. And Toad would lay on a blanket and watch them, as content to be there as the clouds were in the sky.

From Coon Creek, driving to Shawnee Knob took about twenty-five minutes, across the old steel bridge and up a dusty dirt road. The closer the road got to the summit, the narrower and bumpier it became. Dixie rode in the front seat, straddling Toad's lap, with her head out the window, tongue flapping. She seemed eager. Toad wondered if she somehow had an intuition about what would happen.

Boog drove the pickup as far as he could, then parked next to the tree with the Do Not Enter sign that everybody ignored. Justin hopped out of the truck bed, picked up a rock, and hurled it at the sign, hitting it dead center. Toad planted her feet on solid ground to steady herself after the bone-jarring ride. From there, they would have to bushwack about a hundred yards to the lookout. Dixie pissed on both sides of the footpath, then led the way, instinctively knowing where to go. Near the end, they had to step over a fallen tree and through a gap cut in a section of barbed wire fence marking the boundary between private land and the nature preserve. Coon Creekers joked that if those Golden Springs hippies wanted to keep them out, they'd have to build a border wall, because it'd take more than just a wire fence to stop them.

Other than owning a male purebred American boxer with papers to prove it, Toad knew next to nothing about the man she was meeting. When they spoke on the phone, he referred to himself alternately as "Doctor Alolo" or "Professor Alolo," so she thought of him as Doctor Professor Alolo, who had no first name. He used a lot of big words. When they spoke, he said that he was a "visiting resident scholar" at Antaeus College, which sounded to her like a contradiction in terms. Boog said he was probably one of those wiseass professors who taught "Flag Burning 101" or "Introduction to Treason." Toad was a little nervous; she'd never met a liberal before.

A dog barked repeatedly at them when they got close to Shawnee Knob. Toad heard Doctor Professor Alolo command the dog to "desist!" The dog kept barking anyway.

A second person also spoke to the dog. "Whoa, Shabazz, don't be whack, dude!"

Dixie barked back and ran ahead of them.

Who in the heck talks like that? Toad wondered. Rounding a massive oak tree, she saw two black men — one old and cue ball bald, and one young with tangled dreadlocks — standing in the clearing. She hoped they were friendly.

Rufus Cobb had not wanted to do this, but he wasn't about to refuse Mazie a favor. She was ill, she told him, sick to the stomach, maybe with food poisoning or something. *More likely Jell-O shot poisoning*, Rufus thought. But she literally begged him to help her, bent over and clutching her belly, nearly on her knees. Helping her made Rufus feel magnanimous. He hoped she would regard his service as worthy of a return favor.

That didn't mean he was happy to do it, though. Shabazz didn't like him nearly as much as he did Mazie. Specifically, Shabazz didn't seem to like sharing Mazie with Rufus. When the three of them were together, the dog looked at him, drooling, with the corners of his mouth lifted in a snarl to warn him not to make any false moves or risk facing his wrath.

This job promised to be interesting, though. Rufus had never seen a couple of dogs getting it on before, and he'd always wondered if what people called "doggy style" was really how dogs did it. He smoked a joint before reporting for duty, the better to appreciate the novelty of what he would witness.

Rufus had never hiked up to Shawnee Knob. It wasn't as hard as he'd feared, partly because Shabazz pulled him the whole way. He reached the lookout ahead of Professor Alolo, who stopped every few steps to catch his breath. Shabazz pissed on a row of ferns, the canine equivalent of leaving a path of rose petals to the boudoir.

"Congratulations, dude. You're going to get laid today," Rufus told the dog.

Shabazz caught a scent and, excited, barked over and over, ignoring Rufus and Professor Alolo's demands to keep quiet.

Seconds later, the clan from Coon Creek and their bitch came stepping through the brush. Rufus looked at the three of them and felt their eyeballs firing darts all over him. The old lady wore granny glasses, a plaid shawl with tasseled ends, baggy gray pants, and a pair of work boots. The wiry boy with untied shoes, scabbed elbows, and greasy hair made Rufus think of Huckleberry Finn. It was immediately apparent to Rufus that the adult male in this group was strung out. He'd seen more than few junkies in his life and knew what they looked like. The man's jaw hung open sideways, with a dry white tongue beached in his mouth. Rufus noticed that he carried a not-so-concealed Glock under his camouflage jacket.

"You must be Gertrude," Professor Alolo said to the old woman.

"That I am. Call me Toad. I'm pleased to meet you. Doctor Professor Alolo?"

"Indeed."

"This here's my son, Boog."

Boog picked his nose and gurgled, "Sup?"

Boog? Rufus thought. *For real?*

"And my grandson, Justin."

"When do the dogs start humpin' on each other?" Justin asked.

Ignoring the question, Professor Alolo tapped the handle of his cane against Rufus's chest and said, "This is my apprentice, Rufus Cobb."

"Yo." Rufus liked that the Professor had introduced him as his "apprentice," but he still would have preferred to remain anonymous.

Professor Alolo got right down to business. "Have you read the contract?"

"I've got it signed and notarized, right here," Toad said, handing him the paperwork.

Meanwhile, Shabazz was already trying to mount Dixie. Yelping, she wiggled away and retreated to between Toad's legs.

"Chillax, bro!" Rufus hollered, pulling backwards on Shabazz's leash.

"Yah gotta let 'em sniff each other's buttholes," Boog said.

When Shabazz calmed down, Rufus let him off his leash. Happy to be set free, the dog hunkered down on his front legs and lifted his rear, soliciting play. Dixie perked her ears, skeptical but curious. Shabazz snatched a stick in his mouth, shook it a few times, then dropped it at Dixie's paws. She turned it over with her nose. Shabazz circled his tail a couple of times, ran ahead, and turned to look at Dixie, as if to ask, "Are you coming?" She ran to meet him, and they gnawed on each other's necks.

"They need some space," Toad suggested.

Everybody watched without comment while the dogs got to know each other — except for the boy, who regarded Rufus warily out of the corner of one eye. Rufus winked at him. "Yo, yo, yo, my man," he said. "Whassup?"

Justin tried to look away, but once he'd made eye contact, he couldn't break it. "Why'd you do that to your hair?" he asked.

"Justin! Mind your manners," Toad scolded him.

"No prob, Ms. Gertrude. White folks ask me about it all the time." Rufus grabbed a couple of dreadlocks and shook them. "My dreads are a sign of black pride."

"Do you play football? I've seen some football players with hair like that."

"Football players. Rappers. Writers. We're all brothers."

Shabazz and Dixie stopped running together and started nuzzling. They pranced around each other, nipping playfully, then spun in circles together. At once, Dixie stopped and scratched at the ground with her hind legs, clearing the ground beneath her, then wiggled her backside and lifted her tail. Shabazz mounted her and let out an ecstatic yowl.

"Success!" Professor Alolo declared.

"Whoo wee!" Justin exclaimed.

While Shabazz thrusted repeatedly, panting and slobbering, Dixie stood looking straight ahead with a beatific expression, like she was at peace with the world. Their active coupling didn't last long, maybe a minute. Shabazz climaxed anticlimactically; he stiffened for a moment, then just stopped and slid off Dixie's back, briefly getting twisted between his penis and her rear legs in a way that made Rufus wince empathetically. Dixie wiggled to facilitate his dismounting. The dogs then stood butt to butt, still hooked together, and both turned to look back at their humans with eyes half closed and tongues hanging. They looked to Rufus like they could use a cigarette.

PART 2

Left wing, right wing, chicken wing —
It's all the same to me.
Woody Guthrie

CHAPTER 8

When she was in high school, Mazie's proudest achievement hands down was getting a letter to the editor published in the *Coon Creek Citizen Journal*. In it, she criticized her school library for removing the book *Girl, Interrupted* from its collection. Mazie based her argument on three points. First, the librarian did not adhere to due process when she unilaterally removed the book. Second, doing so violated the American Library Association's Bill of Rights: "A person's right to use a library should not be denied or abridged because of origin, age, background, or views." Third, the book had significant literary merit, regardless of how many times its author used the F-word or mentioned blowjobs (in the letter she wrote "sexual situations," but in her mind she meant "blowjobs"), which she cited several positive reviews to establish. Friends and neighbors congratulated her for her skills as a writer, but not, she noticed, for being right.

To Mazie's utter astonishment, the school board subsequently intervened and mandated that the library put *Girl, Interrupted* back on the shelf, albeit with a bright yellow sticker warning parents of "strong language, drug use, suicide, violence, and sexuality." Whatever. Mazie still considered it a personal victory, a harbinger of the great things she could accomplish through a career in writing.

Suddenly, *Girl, Interrupted* was the hottest book in Coon Creek, with a long waiting list to check it out. By the time Mazie finally got her hands on the library's copy, she was outraged to find that somebody had redacted several sections with black marking pen. It was a violation of her inalienable rights. It was a scandal and a cover up. It gave Mazie her first taste of the forbidden fruit of righteous indignation, and it intoxicated her. If that made her a liberal, so what?

Mazie recalled the whole *Girl, Interrupted* incident when she saw a clipping from the *Coon Creek Citizen Journal* stapled to a corkboard in the dormitory. She instantly recognized the Olde English banner and eagle-head logo from the *CJ*s editorial page. She did a double take, hoping that she was wrong. Opinions written beneath that banner nearly always pissed her off. The title of the piece, highlighted with yellow marker, was "Be Proud of Our Pioneer Heritage." She couldn't stop herself from reading:

> *In the wee hours of the night of June 10, while we good folks in Coon Creek were sound asleep, some unknown hooligans snuck into our town and assaulted our civil liberties. Like thieves in the night, these cowards vandalized the statue of our founding father, Philander Fink, right in the heart of the town square. This was not just some prank or juvenile hijinks. No, my friends, this crime was planned in advance by thugs who hate us because of our freedoms and values.*
>
> *We ought never to forget our history. Let the record show that Philander Fink was a truly great man — a frontiersman, an explorer, an entrepreneur, and a born leader — whose*

pioneering spirit was greatly respected in his time, and we remember him today as an inspiration for all of us to live by. If only everybody was so brave and strong! Driven by his passion for adventure, Philander left a comfortable life in Virginia and followed the wilderness road into Kentucky. There he worked as a hired hand on many farms and homesteads to clear the land, plant, and harvest the crops. People said he was one of the most honest and hardest-working young men in the territory. If he had stayed in Kentucky, he could've found a wife and settled down to a nice life.

But that wasn't good enough for our Mister Philander Fink. He loved the life of a trailblazer, so he crossed the Ohio River into the vast woods of an untamed wilderness full of bears, wolves, and Indians. Living off the land, he pushed farther into the wilds than any white man before him. In November of 1801, while exploring a tributary of the upper Little Miami River, he got trapped by an early blizzard and had to hunker down in the back country, alone and far from civilization. Despite the odds against him, he met every challenge and defeated every foe. According to lore, he lived primarily off hunting raccoons — hence, the name of our home, Coon Creek.

Today, while Coon Creekers have gone through more than our fair share of ups and downs, we've always held onto the strength of our founding father. We are all Philander Fink's children.

Thus and so, when those cowards defiled his statue, they also insulted our whole community. They are trying to rewrite history to conform to their silly political correctness. What they don't understand is how we revere Philander Fink, even if he was a white, heterosexual, meat-eating male who carried a firearm. We must stick together. Coon Creekers have every right to be proud of who they are.

With Independence Day coming soon, let's celebrate our freedom in honor of Philander Fink. Let's make Coon Creek great again.

Respectfully, Burl Slocum.

Burl! Upon seeing his name, Mazie easily envisioned him writing that letter. He always did have a way with words, especially when he went off on one of his famous rants. It was one of the things that had attracted Mazie to him, back when they were in high school.

Of course, he also caught her eye with his 6'5", 210 pound linebacker's physique. His supple ass was the subject of frequent discussion among the cheerleaders, but it was Mazie who got up close and personal knowledge of Burl's celebrated glutes. On prom night, she'd dug her fingers so deep into them that she took home some of his skin under her nails. At a purely physical level, despite his Neanderthal opinions and his self-righteous attitude, he was still the best fuck that Mazie had ever known. He'd totally ruined her for normal guys.

In retrospect, Mazie attributed her affair with Burl to a learning experience. They taught each other the pleasures of the flesh in the bed of his pickup during a meteor shower, in the press booth at the stadium during marching-band practice, in the Amity Valley Memorial Gardens at midnight during a thunderstorm, and others. Mazie had to admit that Burl had impressive skills in that department. It made her horny just thinking about it.

The last time she'd seen Burl, though, he'd ballooned out like a beluga whale, which was both a relief and a disappointment to her.

"Hola, Mazie. That's some letter, huh?" El Jefe's scratchy voice burst the bubble of her fantasy.

She wondered how long he'd been watching her. "Whoever wrote that piece of shit is a total asshole," she said.

"True. But this letter, it says a lot about the person who wrote it. He hides his insecurities behind that statue. He thinks that you honor history by living in the past. Still, I'd wager he's not the only person in Coon Creek who feels that way. He isn't writing to convince anybody. He wrote to validate what they already believe."

"He's too stubborn to admit that he's wrong," Mazie said.

"Maybe. But it's better to be believed than to be right."

"What do you mean by that?"

At that moment, Professor Alolo swung open the doors to the seminar room and sang out, "Enter writers. Come, come, come."

The professor seemed to be in a good mood. This puzzled Mazie; she had become accustomed to his irascibility and patronization. She excused these attitudes as by-products of his brilliant creativity. In her experience, happiness and intelligence were inversely related. Seeing Professor Alolo with a shit-eating grin on his face did not jibe with her assumptions about the curse of genius.

Before anybody could sit, Professor Alolo crisscrossed his arms and said, "Get into your groups."

Mazie thought, *Fuck me, not again.*

The Team of Strangers gathered. Rufus high fived El Jefe. Quang gave a thumbs up and opened his laptop. Taara Ali's loose dress swished and briefly covered Rufus's face as she walked past him and sat. The four of them exchanged hugs.

Seriously? Mazie thought. *Hugs?* She lingered at the end of the aisle, pretending to look for something in her purse.

Professor Alolo pointed to group one. "Have you finished your manifesto?"

"We have," replied a tall woman in capri pants and a crop top.

"Read to me its title and the first sentence."

The woman stood tall and read, "'Poets Against Climate Change.' We write the verse for a weeping planet."

"Acceptable," Professor Alolo declared. "Now, go write an ode that will refresh the forests, purify the waters, clear the air, and heal the Earth."

The tall woman bowed her head, as if to a holy man, then returned to her seat.

Professor Alolo faced group two and made a chopping gesture toward them. "Have you finished your manifesto?"

The group members looked around the room, silently assessing who among them would speak first. Finally, a scrawny young man who looked to be no more than sixteen hopped onto his chair and read, "'Silencing Gun Violence.' Every ten seconds, somebody dies from gun violence in America."

Professor Alolo glared at them and said, "Needs work. Don't give me facts and figures. Persuade me with the power of your words. Are you writers or statisticians?"

"Uh, writers," the lad stammered.

"Then write a story that readers will feel like a bullet to the heart."

Next, Professor Alolo turned to the Team of Strangers and asked, "What do you have for me?"

El Jefe stood and spoke: "'Toward a People's History.' To change people's hearts and minds, you must expose the false narratives of history."

"Explain," Professor Alolo said.

"History is a fiction written by an elite few to justify the status quo. Monuments are put up by the vested powers to perpetuate that fiction. By their nature, they are oppressive."

"That's true," Professor Alolo affirmed. "I've written on that subject myself."

Rufus jumped to his feet. "And professor," he continued, "We're keeping it real, 'cause we're writing about a monument that's standing right now in the public square in a nearby town."

"Excellent," Professor Alolo pronounced. "Write as if you're tearing down that monument with your words."

The Team of Strangers nodded in satisfaction. Mazie too, despite her doubts about this project. She agreed with the idea in general, but not so much the specifics. Messing with the statue of Philander Fink was a good way to get shot in Coon Creek. Surely they could find a safer target to make their point, like the statue of Christopher Columbus at the statehouse or the confederate soldier memorial in Franklin County. They seemed fixated on Philander Fink, though.

Professor Alolo folded his arms and puffed his chest. It looked to Mazie like the pose he'd assumed on the dust jacket photo of *Impossible to Underestimate*. Now, though, fifty years later, he looked more like a defiant scarecrow than a dangerous revolutionary. She also noticed the outline of a flask in his pants pocket.

When he finished interrogating the groups, Professor Alolo asked, "So what are you all waiting for?" He snapped his fingers. "Start writing."

The Team of Strangers huddled up. Fingers poised above his laptop keyboard, Quang asked, "Are we ready?"

"Ready. Always. For anything," Taara said.

"Being ready is not the same as knowing what to do," El Jefe remarked.

"This is how writing should always be! No rules! No restrictions! We can just let our creative juices flow," Quang gushed. He typed his own words as he spoke them, complete with exclamation marks.

"But this won't be easy. The professor has some weird-ass ideas," Rufus said.

Listening to them, Mazie wondered if she could get traded to another team. She muttered "balderdash," which, she immediately realized to her horror, was the word her mother substituted for "bullshit." That bothered her, so she modified her comment to, "Oh, fuck."

"What fuck?" Rufus patted her hand; he looked at her with a deep-eyed expression of concern. "You seem kind of cranky today."

Now everybody looked at her, and all she wanted to do was disappear. This feeling triggered her default defense mechanism, which was to counterattack.

"We don't need any fucking manifesto. I don't give a rat's ass about a rusty statue of an old dead white hillbilly in some bass-ackwards shithole of a small town in the middle of nowhere. That place, Coon Creek, is like its stupid statue: stuck, standing there watching the world pass it by and powerless to do anything to change it. If the statue of Philander fucking Fink came to life, he'd feel right at home there. People's attitudes haven't changed in two hundred years."

Mazie immediately regretted what she'd said. It was way too personal. Wasn't a catharsis supposed to make you feel better? Instead, she felt like she'd just lost control of her bowels in front of everybody. Passion was a filthy thing.

"I'm sorry," she said. "All I want to do is write."

El Jefe murmured "hmmmm" with an ascending inflection, like he was rising up to catch a thought. When he got it, he tapped his hand against the armrest of his seat. "That's it!"

"That's a really dope idea, Maze," Rufus cut in. "Imagine if that statue did come to life after two centuries. What would it do? What would it think? How would people react? Damn, I think that's a story just waiting for us to write."

Yeah, Mazie thought. *That's actually a pretty cool idea.* She took out her cell phone, opened a notepad, and started tapping in words, saying them aloud as she did:

"It can go something like this....

"Philander Fink, feeling stiff, achy, and hungover, awakened in a strange place, with no memory of the previous night. He'd drank heavily and could only hope that he hadn't made a total ass of himself again.

But why was he standing on a pedestal in the middle of a park, with a pigeon on his head and a rifle on his shoulder? He looked around and saw he was still in Coon Creek, but somehow everything looked different."

"That's what I'm talking about!" Rufus said. "Let's roll with that idea. So, what does he see?"

"Filth, ignorance, desperation." Mazie said. "He sees overflowing garbage cans, trash blowing in the wind, squalid puddles of oily water, junk cars parked in front of boarded-up houses, and, in the middle of it all, the blackened shell of a bereft, burned-out factory, a bleak cathedral to the people's despair, which showed in the dull blankness of their faces."

Team Stranger listened to her in rapt admiration.

"Epic!" Rufus extolled. "You nailed it."

El Jefe asked, "Have you ever been to that place, Coon Creek?"

"Never in this life," Mazie replied.

The hardest thing to get used to was how quiet it got during the evenings in Golden Springs. It was scary. Around sundown things started to get lively in Rufus's hood on the east side of Cleveland. He grew up in a duplex with the railroad tracks as his backyard and an alley for his front yard, near the corner of Kinsman and E. 93rd Street, where the incessant noises of the city formed the soundtrack of his youth. He used to sit on the crumbling porch by the side entrance to his home and bask in the constant whoosh, rumble, and screech, punctuated by sirens, shots, screams, and collisions. He marveled at how every day's eclectic cacophony was totally unique. Listening made his senses sharper, his thoughts more alert. Cleveland spoke to him in rugged verse. He fell asleep every night to the drum and pulse of the streets.

As soon as he graduated from the University of Toledo with a degree in education, he returned to East Cleveland with a mission—to teach poetry to the children of the city. He wanted to be the teacher he wished he'd had, so he took his students on field trips downtown to listen to the urban music. He stood with them on street corners, where they shouted their poetry at the tops of their lungs for passersby to hear. He urged his student to "live poetry out loud," to fill people's headspace with art, for free.

Golden Springs, however, had its own built-in volume control.

Sitting with Shabazz inside a gazebo near the alumni house, Rufus worried that the silence might wipe his brain clean. Too much quiet made him restless. How could a poet work in such an audible void? It made him feel like he was drowning. Or, maybe he felt like that because he was extraordinarily stoned.

Rufus scratched Shabazz behind the ears and said, "I'm kind of freaking out."

Shabazz barked—it sounded like "*yes.*" Rufus wondered if he'd heard right. The dog started wagging his tail so fast it blurred like a propeller. Rufus imagined Shabazz taking flight.

"Somebody's glad to see me," Mazie said, approaching from the main path.

Rufus stood and smiled broadly when he saw her. Mazie walked past him and rubbed Shabazz's rump. *Shit,* he thought. *I wish I had a tail.*

Rufus shushed her. "Listen. Check it out, how quiet it is. Like being on the moon."

Mazie looked past Rufus to the alumni house, where the curtains to Professor Alolo's office were closed. "You're high, aren't you?"

Rufus winced. "Just a little bit." He held his thumb and pointer finger in front of him, with just a tiny space between them.

Mazie clicked her tongue. Shabazz squirmed in front of her, as if he couldn't decide which part of his body to present for her to pet. Watching the dog made Rufus dizzy. He steadied himself by latching onto Mazie's shoulder.

"Easy, boy," she said.

Rufus wondered if she meant him or the dog.

"So, what's going on?" Mazie asked. "Why are you here?"

"Yeah, uh, see, Professor Alolo kicked me out. He said that he was busy and didn't want to be disturbed. So, he asked me to hand Shabazz over to you for his evening walk."

Mazie took the leash from Rufus's hand. "Okay, thanks."

Before she could get away, Rufus asked, "Mind if I tag along?"

She took a deep breath and exhaled with a single word, "Sure."

Shabazz led them. Nose to the ground, the dog sniffed a route that took them off the main path, behind the fine arts building, under a windmill, into the Golden Springs Nature Preserve, and up the hill. Mazie and Rufus hustled to keep up with him.

"Shabazz seems in a hurry," Mazie remarked.

"I think he wants to go to Shawnee Knob," Rufus said. "I'm cool with taking a hike. You?"

"What Shabazz wants, Shabazz gets," Mazie panted.

Not watching where he was going, Rufus stubbed his toe against a tree root and tripped forward, skipping and flailing his arms to keep from falling, and stomping through a patch of wild ginger in the process.

"Oops," he said.

"You're kind of clumsy, aren't you?"

"Busted!" Rufus raised his arms. "I'm easily distracted."

"Distracted by what?" Mazie asked.

Rufus thought, By *your earlobes*. He simultaneously fantasized about and restrained himself from leaning forward to nibble on them.

"Just stuff," he replied, hoping she wouldn't ask for details.

To his relief, though, Shabazz wasn't slowing down, which made it impossible for them to sustain a conversation. Rufus had a million memes flashing through his mind, but not a single intelligible thought. Nothing is more impotent than a poet at a loss for words. His fear of silence was coming back. The more they walked, the harder it became for him to think of something unfoolish to say.

"You're sweating," Mazie observed.

Oh shit, Rufus thought. *I must stink.*

"Would you like a drink of water?" She offered him her water bottle.

"Yes. Please."

"Sure. I brought it for the dog, but you look like you need it more."

Mazie pitched the bottle to Rufus; he caught it, twisted open the cap, and gulped without breaking stride. He thought of Mazie's lips touching the top of the bottle, her tongue licking the rim.

"Hey, by the way, I wanted to tell you something," he said and handed back the bottle. "Yo, you were really on fire today in class. I mean, the way you described that Podunky little town was spot on."

Mazie flinched. "I'm a writer. That's what I do."

"You nailed the little details. The potholes so big that ducks swim in them. Tennis shoes strung by their laces over telephone wires. The plastic flowers in the planters at the mobile home park. People wearing their pajamas at the laundromat. I love it."

"Thanks." Mazie tipped her shoulder at him. "I live in Columbus, but I know a lot of people that live like peasants in poor, dirty, shitty little towns just like that one. The funny thing is they're proud of it."

"Yeah, I kind of feel sorry for them."

"Bullshit," Mazie quickly replied.

Rufus bristled. Had he said something stupid?

"I'm telling you that the one thing you can say that pisses them off more than anything is that you feel sorry for them."

"Yo, I get it."

"No, you don't."

"But I do. I sure enough do, 'cause of the way you write about it."

"Oh. Well, I appreciate you saying so."

Rufus felt his cheeks throb; he was black blushing.

Mazie continued, "And I never told you, Rufus, but I thought that was a pretty cool stunt you guys pulled with that stupid statue."

"Too bad you couldn't come."

They reached the summit of Shawnee Knob sooner than Rufus would've liked. When the clearing came into sight, Shabazz started prancing in frantic circles around Mazie's legs, getting twisted up in the leash.

"Why not let him run?" Rufus suggested.

"Okay," she said and dropped the leash.

Shabazz hightailed it to the overlook, barking joyously. Mazie and Rufus slowed to a relaxed pace, taking small steps, drifting from side to side, brushing against each other. High overhead, the canopy of oak leaves soughed in a ghost wind. They stepped into the clearing just as the setting sun touched the horizon. Its aura imbued the valley with vivid tawny colors. Orange rays of light fanned across both sides of Clifton Gorge, casting bright ripples off Elixir Creek in the foreground and lengthening the shadows of the Coon Creek boulder field in the distance. Rufus and Mazie paused to reflect.

Rufus angled his head a few degrees toward Mazie, thinking that if she turned to look at him at that exact moment, he'd make a move to kiss her, or at least ask if he could kiss her, since he'd always heard that rich white chicks were all about consent. All it would take was a glance....

Shabazz made a sound they'd never heard from him before, deflecting Mazie from her reverie and Rufus from his intentions. The dog was on its back, belly up and legs splayed, rolling in the ground at the exact spot where he and Dixie had mated, whinnying like a drunk horse.

"What's wrong with Shabazz?" Mazie asked.

"I think he's in love," Rufus guessed.

By the time she got back to her room, Mazie felt anxious, like the way she'd felt as a little girl and she'd done something wrong but nobody knew it yet. The blended sensation left her rubber legged with worry, hollow stomached with remorse, dizzy headed with apprehension... but also tingly all over her skin with the possibility that she just might get away with something and suffer no ill consequences.

When parting from Rufus, he'd told her that he had a "really good time," as if they'd gone on a date and not just walked the dog. She simply said "yeah," but did not specify whether she agreed that she, too, had a good time, or that she knew he'd had a good time. Mazie didn't mean to lead him on, but he was so willing to be led that it almost seemed like she did him a favor by acting coy. Playing hard to get was a new kick for her.

But Mazie understood that the deeper source of her guilty titillation was deprecating her hometown and mocking her own people. She felt like a child using a forbidden curse word. Sure, Coon Creek was a dump and she'd be fine if she never set foot there again, but it was one thing to feel that way and another to say it out loud. Maybe she'd grown "too big for her britches," just like her mother had warned her.

Mazie felt so uncomfortable with this feeling that she had to do something to get rid of it, without admitting anything, and there was only one person whom she trusted enough to lie to. She went to the library to use the phone there. She dialed the land line, rather than the cell phone. She counted the rings, determined to quit on the fourth.

"Hello?" Toad answered on the other end.

The sound of her mother's voice traveled from her ear straight to the pit of her stomach, where it landed like a bomb, sending shock waves of guilt to all corners of her body and a great mushroom cloud into her throat. She could not have spoken a word if she'd wanted to. Mazie hung up.

CHAPTER 9

Meredith bought a copy of the *Golden Springs Gazette* and a Clif Bar at a mini-mart on the way out of town. The local, independent, nonprofit newspaper reported "news you need" from the Golden Springs and Antaeus College communities, including all social, civic, ecological, commercial, political, and cultural affairs; it even had a sports section, although they limited its coverage to nonprofessional, noncompetitive sports not linked to brain injuries. Golden Springers generally considered anything written in the *Gazette* to be gospel. Meredith, not so much.

"Hope the news is good," the clerk at the mini-mart said to her.

"Is it ever?" Meredith replied, leaving the clerk confused and speechless. She folded the paper, stuffed it into her backpack, and tossed it onto the passenger seat of her Smart car.

Ever since their first trip to Coon Creek, Meredith had made regular junkets there to purchase pies for Roscoe Alolo. It seemed to her like a hospitable thing to do, although the more pie trips that she made just for him, the closer she got to the limits of her hospitality. Sure, she had a vested interest in keeping him happy, but she was a colleague, after all, not his personal pie supplier.

Despite her misgivings, Meredith considered this a prudent solution. Professor Alolo loved his pies, and he became noticeably petulant if he went more than a day without his favorite dessert. Not just any pie was good enough, though; he demanded none less than the award-winning pies baked exclusively at the Hungry Coon Diner. Unfortunately, his passion for those pies available nowhere-else-in-the-world conflicted with his principled refusal to set foot in Coon Creek. If it meant that Meredith would have to go there herself to fetch the pies, it was a small enough price to pay in the name of peaceful coexistence.

Besides, Meredith sort of liked getting out of Golden Springs occasionally. It took her mind off her personal problems. She enjoyed the drive past green rolling hills, horses grazing in pastures, fields of corn planted in perfectly straight rows, and even the Chew Mail Pouch Tobacco barn. These, and many other aspects of Midwestern Gothic, secretly appealed to her, things like playing cornhole, saying "dontcha know," tipping cows, making fried-baloney sandwiches, and pouring ranch dressing on top of everything. Before moving to Ohio, she thought that such things were just dumb stereotypes; now, she found them kind of, well, charming.

Too bad that charm was completely lost on Vanessa. She made it very clear that she wanted nothing to do with Ohio.

After crossing the steel bridge, Meredith rounded a sharp bend along Coon Creek, and straight ahead of her was the landmark that campus folks mockingly referred to as the "Good Old Boy Billboard." It lined up with her steering wheel like the cross hairs in a target. Its words read: "God is watching when you vote."

Standing next to it was a tall cross, with words along each axis:

<pre>
              R
      BELVEDERE
              V
              E
              R
              E
              N
              D
</pre>

And beneath it was a banner with the words: For Mayor.

Meredith hit the brakes and stopped in the middle of the road to make sure she was seeing correctly. The notion that God endorsed a mayoral candidate seemed outrageous, even for good old boys. She wasn't sure whether it was meant to be taken literally, or if it perhaps contained some kind of right-wing code or double entendre. She took a photo of it with her cell phone.

A boy around thirteen years old piloted a John Deere riding mower in a pattern of concentric squares through the field surrounding the billboard. Meredith waved at him. The boy shot her a gap-toothed grin and double-barreled middle fingers.

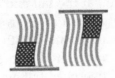

Faye Pfeiffer knew the precise moment when Edith Doody took the afternoon pies out of the oven. On Mondays, Wednesdays, and Fridays, when Edith baked pecan pies, Faye religiously arrived at the Hungry Coon Diner ahead of time to get hers while they were still hot. While waiting, she sat at the counter and drank black coffee.

"Good to see you, hon," Edith chirped at Faye when she entered. "The pies will be ready in a jiffy."

Sometimes when Edith wasn't especially busy, she'd chat with Faye about her favorite subjects, "this, that, and the other thing." But she was keeping an eye on the oven, so Faye smoothed her trousers and sat down on a stool by the counter.

"Take your time, Mrs. Doody. I'll just sit here and sip my coffee."

The only time that Faye ever drank coffee was when she was at the Hungry Coon Diner, and then only one cup. Too much caffeine made her tap her toes and twiddle her thumbs. Drinking coffee, though, provided cover for her real purpose, which was to watch people. Most days, she had no human contact, save for the dead or grieving. It did her good to get out of the mortuary occasionally to participate in the affairs of the living, if only as an observer, and the Coon Creek Diner was the place to go for that. Edith Doody was a reliable source for current events and juicy rumors, which usually satisfied Faye's need for animate human contact.

It was 1:30 p.m., at the tail end of the lunch hour. Folks lingering in the diner sat in front of their pushed-aside empty plates and chatted with each other, or just sat by themselves and stared into space. A lethargic ceiling fan plodded overhead but generated no relief to the day's heat whatsoever.

"Hot enough for yah?" Edith asked.

"It's tepid," Faye replied.

"Maybe to you it's just tepid. Holy baloney, I don't know how you can stand it, always wearin' that dark suit and tie. How do you do it without ever even breakin' a sweat?"

Actually, as a teenager, Faye often got damp when nervous, worried, or stressed. She'd learned to control her perspiration by dint of sheer willpower.

"It comes with the job," she said.

Faye observed that Edith wore a Belvedere for Mayor button on her apron. "I see that you support the reverend's campaign," she commented.

"Well, I ain't got nothin' against Mayor Ball. But things haven't been goin' too good here in Coon Creek. I've always voted for the Democrats, 'cause they usually have a workin' person's back. Maybe it's time to go Republican, though. Gotta shake things up. Reverend Belvedere is a good man."

"Yes, and a godly man," Faye agreed.

"Well, alrighty then. D'yah want a button for your own? I got a whole bag of them back of the cash register."

"Uh, I don't...." Faye changed what she was going to say when she saw Edith reach into the bag. "Well, I could wear it when I'm not working, I suppose."

"Here yah go, then," Edith said, handing her the button.

Faye cupped it with her hand and said, "Thanks."

"Now, I'd better go check on them pies," Edith said. She scurried through the double doors and into the kitchen.

Faye sipped her coffee; it was already cold.

The front door to the Hungry Coon Diner had a distinctive squeak. Edith could have oiled it, but she'd come to count on it to alert her when a new customer entered. Regulars at the diner knew to open and shut the door a couple of times to make sure she knew they'd arrived. By contrast, whenever out-of-towners visited, they'd hear the squeak and stop pushing, as if they'd done something wrong, and then they'd open the door very slowly, trying to be discreet.

Faye looked up when she heard that squeak, as did everybody else, and turned to see who had just come in. A black woman Faye had never seen before stood in the doorway. Customers in the diner looked at her once, then returned to what they were doing — except Faye, who couldn't look away.

Dressed in an off-white boiler suit, with a floral scarf, multiple bracelets, and sporting short and slicked-back hair, the woman looked unkempt and elegant at the same time. She took uneven steps: one long stride left, a short one right, while keeping her back stiff. She had a backpack slung over her shoulder, with a rolled-up newspaper sticking out of an outside pocket. Her eyes darted side to side, as if she was doing math in her head. In the fleeting second that the woman and Faye exchanged glances, she nodded and half smiled.

The woman went straight to the cash register. When nobody immediately acknowledged her, she looked around the counter, into the kitchen.

Edith Doody came, drying her hands on her apron. "Oh, it's you Professor Stokes. Back for some more pies, are yah?"

The woman replied, "Call me Meredith. And indeed I am."

"Can't get enough, eh? Even y'all from the wine and cheese side of Clifton Gorge like a good pie, eh? What'll it be for yah today?"

Faye listened intently, trying to piece together the bits of information the conversation revealed.

"I want three pies, please. Dutch apple, very berry. And praline pecan."

"I can fix yah up with the apple and berry pies, Meredith. But I'm feared that I cain't do yah the pecan pie. I only got one comin' out of the oven, and it's already spoken for." Edith pointed down the counter straight at Faye. Meredith's eyes followed the line.

Without thinking, Faye said, "Oh, that's quite alright. She can have the pie."

Meredith shook her head. "No, no. I couldn't."

But having surprised herself by speaking up, Faye committed to following through with the offer. She told herself that she didn't want it anymore.

"Please," Faye implored her. "I insist. Really. You came all this way. I can get another pie. It will mean more to me if you take it." She wanted to slap herself when she spoke those words. She meant what she said, but when she replayed them in her mind, she felt like a child trying to please an adult.

Meredith stepped forward, bouncing slightly on her heels. "That's so very kind of you." She put her hand on Faye's shoulder. "My name is Meredith Stokes."

"Faye. Faye Pfeiffer."

"Well, Faye Pfeiffer, thank you so much. I owe you a favor."

Meredith brushed shoulders against Faye as she walked away. She took the pies and carried them in stacked boxes out the door. The last thing she did before leaving was smile at Faye.

Faye turned liquid. She felt her soul flush out of her and swirl down the drain. For several seconds, she stared at the door, hoping but not hoping that Meredith Stokes would return. Finally, Faye blinked away jumbled thoughts and noticed a newspaper on the floor. It must have fallen out of Meredith's pack when she brushed against her. Faye hopped off the stool, grabbed the paper, and hurried out the door, just in time to see Meredith drive away in a tiny car that looked like an egg. Faye looked at the bumper stickers on the back of the car as it pulled away: Coexist, Darwin fish, Visualize Peace, and I'm Pro-Choice and I Vote. Largest of all, an iridescent rainbow flag decal covered the length of the rear hatch window.

Faye watched until the car turned off Main Street and onto Route 343. As soon as it was out of sight, she felt a bubble rise from her stomach, into her throat, and fill her mouth with a bitter taste. At the same time, the faint hairs on her shoulders tingled. She started sweating under her arms. Disgust and arousal were a volatile emotional brew.

When the sensation passed, Faye clicked her tongue. She still had the newspaper tucked under her arm. Returning to the diner, Faye ordered a piece of rhubarb pie, drank her black coffee, and read the newspaper.

Burl Slocum's first principle of good dietary health was that the body required constant nourishment. Thus, rather than the customary three meals per day, Burl's daily intake included designated midmorning, midafternoon, before-bed, and midnight snacks. If he missed any one of those, his mental and emotional well-being quickly declined. He generally took his midafternoon repast at the Hungry Coon Diner.

"Tuesday usual?" Edith asked when Burl arrived at the diner.

"It's Tuesday, isn't it?"

The second principle of Burl's regimen was that adhering to a consistent menu for each day of the week helped to promote equilibrium. On Tuesdays, Burl dined on swine; hence, his midafternoon mainstay was a pulled pork sandwich platter.

Burl also valued regularity in his personal habits, so for each day of the week, he sat in a different booth at the diner. This provided him with both consistency and variety. Folks knew his proclivities so well that nobody sat in Burl's prescribed booth on its designated day, and Edith had his place set before he even showed up. As Burl took his seat in his Tuesday booth, he noticed a newspaper that somebody had left behind on the counter; he snatched it and took it with him.

Edith brought the coffee pot. "That fancy pie lady from Golden Springs was here and dropped that on her way out the door. Ever since, customers have been passing it around."

"Is that so?" Burl unfurled the paper while Edith poured his coffee.

It had been a long time since Burl had read the *Golden Springs Gazette*. It always aggravated him because it was a tool of the leftist media, but it occasionally amused him in the same way that watching somebody slip on a banana peel was funny.

Only in Golden Springs would free massages, a candlelight vigil for the Dalai Lama, or meeting notes from the Diversity Book Club make the headlines. What a bunch of rubes!

Edith brought Burl's platter. "Any good news in there?" she asked.

"Yes. Good for nothing."

Burl chewed vigorously while reading. He skimmed headlines, then read a paragraph or two before deciding if an article was worth his time. On the editorial page, a headline caught his eye, "To Embrace the Future, Purge the Past." He stopped chewing, the better to focus. He disagreed with it so ardently that he couldn't quit reading, much as he'd have liked to. It was another one of those self-righteous rants written by an elitist asshole who thought he knew better than everybody else. This was just more proof to Burl's theory that there was a direct correlation between higher education and idiotic opinions. It made Burl proud of his high school education.

When he finished his lunch, Burl took the newspaper with him. He had an idea he wanted to try out on a certain gang of people, and he knew just where to find them.

Boog started drinking earlier than usual that day. At the Drink Here Tavern, the definitions of early and late in respect to drinking were related to one's employment status, conflicting obligations, and the amount of time passed since the last drink. For any person with no job, nothing to do, and four or more hours of sleep since the last drink, there was really no reason to wait until 5:00 p.m. In fact, by the standards of a large percentage of the adult male population of the town, Boog was way behind in his drinking when he drifted into the tavern at 2:00 p.m.

There was already a quorum of the Galoots in the tavern. Buzz Pringle and Paddy O'Brien were arm wrestling to a stalemate; neither seemed to be trying too hard. Tank Turner was singing "Like a Rock" with the jukebox. Red Ryan was watching the *$100,000 Pyramid* on the television behind the bar, shouting at it, "Rooster Cogburn, damnit, the answer is Rooster Cogburn." Burl Slocum filled a booth by himself. And Boog's old man sat quietly at the bar, face down in a schooner of Iron City.

Boog sidled onto the stool next to Zeke and ordered a pitcher. "Sup, Dad? Don't usually see you hereabouts this time of day."

"What freakin' difference does it make?"

"Whoa, Dad. Something bugging you?"

"I got blood in my piss."

"Is that so? Well, I'd be lying if I said that wasn't bad. But it might not be no more than some itty-bitty infection. Buzz had some such bug last year." Boog hollered across the room, "Hey Buzz, what'd you do last year when you was pissing blood?"

"I drank a lot of cranberry juice," Buzz replied.

While Buzz was distracted, Paddy leaned with all his might into his forearm and defeated him in their arm-wrestling contest.

"No fair!" Buzz protested.

"Was so!" Paddy maintained.

Ignoring the fracas, Boog said to his father, "See what I mean? All you gotta do is flush out your bladder."

"Not so," Zeke said. "The doctor says I've got kidney stones."

"Ouch. Sorry about that, Dad. I heard that's kinda painful when they pass."

"That's why I'm drinkin'." Zeke sighed, then added, "Goddamn that fucking Hercules Steel plant for doing this to me. I oughta sue their asses."

Boog had heard his old man's harangue against the company a thousand times before. To hear him tell it, every sniffle or wart he'd had in the last decade was due to some toxic substance he'd ingested while working at the mill. Zeke believed that he was part of some diabolical government experiment on human subjects.

While Boog was no fan of the Hercules Steel Company, he shrugged at the old man's paranoid theories, because even if they were true, they were still far less menacing than the many and varied deep-state schemes that rich liberals were hatching to ruin the country by taking his guns and starting a war against religion.

"Hey up, Boog. Get on over here."

Boog didn't have to look up to recognize Tank Turner's drunken roar. "Stop your quacking back there," he retorted.

The Galoots were now all seated around one table, as if gathered for a summit meeting. Boog excused himself to his father and went to join them. "What's got you goobers all worked up about today?" he asked them as he pulled up a chair.

Red passed a newspaper to Buzz, who passed it to Paddy, who unfolded it and smoothed it out on the table, then passed it to Boog.

"What's this?" Boog squinted to read the headline. "Why're you dipshits reading this rag from Golden Springs? Ain't nothing in it but lies."

"Just read this one letter," Tank said, tapping his finger on the page to show Boog where to start. "And get ready to blow chunks."

The headline was, "To Embrace the Future, Purge the Past."

Reading in front of people made Boog feel self-conscious, but he didn't want to let the Galoots down. He cleared his throat and began to read slowly, pausing to sound out the big words.

> *The history of civilization reveals that cultural memory is selective. Societies fabricate a civic folklore that binds their populace through the willful aggrandizement of quintessential shared values....*

"What in the fuck does this mean?" Boog cried.

"Just keep reading," Tank urged. "Don't matter if you cain't understand all of them words. Yah'll understand enough."

Boog picked up where he left off.

> *When, however, the contrived mythology masks ignoble truths, the vox populi must be deconstructed, investigated, acknowledged, and repudiated so the commonwealth can evolve to meet the moral challenges of modernity.*

"Whoever wrote this had a bad case of diarrhea of the mouth," Boog declared, taking a break from the strain of reading. "I don't know what every other word even means."

"Yah ain't even got to the best part yet," Tank said.

Consider, for example, the case of one Philander Fink, who is revered as a hero in a certain neighboring hamlet. There, the prevailing narrative surrounding this man, Fink, depicts him as a courageous frontiersman, a visionary entrepreneur, and a role model for subsequent generations. Such is Fink's glorified stature that his likeness, in the form of a bronze statue, has stood in the central plaza of that community for several decades.

The factual history of Fink tells a very different story. My research has revealed that, rather than to quench a thirst for high adventure, Fink migrated west of the Appalachian Mountains to escape burdensome gambling debts in Baltimore.

Unfortunately, soon after he arrived in Kentucky, Fink imprudently accrued ever greater liabilities in the taverns and brothels of backwoods towns. Inasmuch as his notorious reputation rendered him incapable of securing legitimate employment, he became a bounty hunter. He specialized in surreptitiously crossing the Ohio River into lawless territories where he could track and apprehend escaped slaves, whom he returned, in chains, to their overlords, to be tortured or killed. Over time, Fink acquired the calumnious notoriety of being one of the most proficient slave catchers in all of Kentucky.

Contrary to the sanitized legends about this man, Fink was a scoundrel, a miscreant, a wretch, and a ruffian, who in his day was shunned and reviled by all decent people. It is only through gross distortion of historical fact that he is today held in undeserved regard.

Therefore, upon discovery of these truths, it is incumbent upon modern people of goodwill to correct past sins. We must denounce the felon, Philander Fink. We must topple the statue of him that stands in Coon Creek.

Urgently, Roscoe Alolo.

"Where in the flaming fuck did you get this?" Boog thundered.

"Burl gave it to me," Tank said.

"Who in the hell is this Ros-cunt Ass-hole-lo?" Buzz asked.

"Oh, he's some la-de-da professor at Antaeus College," Boog told him.

"We cain't just let this stand," Red asserted.

"This is war!" Paddy agreed.

Hearing this, Burl Slocum stepped out of his booth and butted in as if he'd been waiting for just the right moment. "I've got an idea. Hear me out...."

Mazie took Shabazz along with her on her morning jog. Surprisingly, although Shabazz was unruly when walking on his leash, he behaved well when jogging, trotting alongside Mazie as deftly as a dance partner. Whenever she slowed down, he gently nudged her to pick up the pace. It felt like having a personal trainer.

Mazie jogged the same route every morning: from Bard Hall, down the main path, along Campus Drive, and by the nature preserve, until she reached Golden Springs, where she went up Main Street to the end of town, then back the same way. Up before 6:00 a.m., she often saw nary a soul in the time it took to complete the entire circuit. The solitude and her steady pace encouraged a pleasant mindlessness.

It was a Tuesday morning. As was her routine, she jogged to the town limits, then turned around to return. Shabazz pulled back on the leash, barking and refusing to go along with her.

"Shut up," Mazie scolded. "You'll wake up the whole town."

This was not Shabazz's typical happy-to-be-a-dog bark, nor was it his don't-mess-with-me bark. This sounded more like a look-at-me bark. "What's the matter?" she asked him.

Shabazz dragged Mazie forward to the sign that welcomed visitors to Golden Springs. Only it wasn't Golden *Springs* anymore. Overnight, somebody had dislodged the letters of the word Springs and replaced it with a new word, stenciled and spray painted: Showers.

Welcome to Golden Showers.

And that wasn't all. The water supply for the three-tiered waterfall fountain had been dyed bright yellow.

Mazie thought, *This prank has Burl Slocum's signature all over it.* Who else would've concocted something so vile and irreverent, and yet so funny. Welcome to Golden Showers, indeed.

CHAPTER 10

Mazie closed her eyes to encourage elusive ideas out of hiding. In the darkness behind her eyelids, fragments of a story began to fall into place. She hovered her fingers above the keyboard, prepared to capture them in words as soon as they coalesced in her mind. She could almost reach out and grab them....

Three sharp knocks on the door scattered her inner visions just moments before she could grab them. She groaned in frustration.

"Yo, yo, yo, Maze," Rufus called from the other side of the door. "C'mon. The team is meeting in the lounge."

"*Fuck me*," Mazie muttered under her breath. Even though the summer literary program advertised that it would "encourage, nurture, enlighten, and inspire emerging writers," in fact it created an environment full of niggling distractions that prevented her *from* writing. She stared at the door and imagined it bursting into flames.

"Are you in there, Mazie?"

Mostly, she just wanted to be left alone. Still, a small part of her wanted to answer him; she would have liked to confess her frustrations to somebody, and Rufus was her most likely confidant. Neither wanting to encourage him nor tempt herself, she covered her mouth and pretended she wasn't in the room.

"Okay. That's dope. I guess you ain't in there," Rufus said. "I'll come back and check on you later."

If truly he believed she wasn't in the room, why did he say that? Maybe Rufus was more perceptive than she'd originally given him credit for.

Now, though, she was stuck. She couldn't leave the room until she was sure nobody would see her, not even to go to the bathroom, which, suddenly, she felt the urgent need to do. And she could forget about writing. Nobody ever wrote anything worth reading while they had to take a piss. Mazie crossed her legs and waited.

Taara Ali blew her top, launching to her feet and declaring "I am outraged!" with such a furious expression on her face that her hijab slipped and corkscrews of frizzy hair sprang loose.

"We all are," El Jefe said. "If you're not, you aren't paying attention. I've been outraged over this, that, or something else most of my life. Little good it has done for me. My grandfather said to me that Americans will believe anything except the truth. I used to wonder what he meant by that. Now, I think I understand."

Rufus removed a handful of envelopes from a folder that he'd brought to the meeting and waved them for the others to see. "This is just some of the hate mail that Professor Alolo has received since he wrote that editorial. He read each letter and just laughed and tossed them in the trash, like he was totally unfazed by them, even kind of pleased. But I picked them out. Listen up to the load of bullshit these dumb crackers are writing to him:

> *'Philander Fink would kick your ratty black ass.'*
>
> *'Your momma wishes that she could "purge the past" so she'd never met your poppa.'*
>
> *'You're so full of shit that you have to use a tarp instead of toilet paper.'*
>
> *'Your balls would look good floating in my beer.'*
>
> *'Does it hurt to have such a long hard pole up your ass?'*
>
> *'I'm drunk. What's your excuse for being so ignorant?'*

"And those are just a few. There are also a ton of 'die' letters—die commie, die faggot, die nigger, eat shit and die, don't die before I can kill you... and such and so on."

"That's harsh," Quang said.

"Very nasty," El Jefe agreed. "But kind of funny, in a sick redneck way."

"We much must defend the professor against this slander!" Taara insisted. "The men who wrote these things, they are obviously *racists!*"

"Well, duh," Rufus concurred.

"Listen to me." El Jefe sighed wearily. "It does no good to call somebody a racist. They will always deny it. Nobody thinks that they're racist. If you were to ask the Grand Imperial Bozo of the Ku Klux Klan, he would swear on his Bible that he's not a racist. The funny thing is that most racists think they themselves are victims of racism. Ignorance makes everybody a victim.

"All my life, people have called me Cheech, or Taco, or Wetback, because they think I'm Mexican. But I am Cuban. Are these people racist? Yes, certainly. But to them being Cuban, Mexican, Colombian, or from any Spanish-speaking nation is all the same—they are distinctions without a difference. Ignorance cares nothing for details, or for the truth.

"But the sad thing is that racists need people like us, they just don't know it. They need somebody to blame for all the things they fuck up. Racism is a substitute for self-loathing. Having a scapegoat means never having to admit making a mistake.

"You can't fix racists. Don't bother trying. The best you can do is fix their mistakes so they can't poison other people's minds."

Quang had taken notes on his tablet the whole time El Jefe spoke. Rufus had mumbled "uh huh" and "right on" to every point El Jefe made.

Tara stomped her feet and snapped, "We, too, deserve to have scapegoats!"

"Damn straight," Rufus concurred. "So, that brings us back to the reason we are meeting here today. We need to strike back. But we need to plan it very carefully."

Taara: "Oh yes. We are going to do it!"

Quang: "I'm in. It sounds like fun."

El Jefe: "Yes, we should." He unfolded his legs and straightened in his chair. "But where is Mazie? Is she with us or against us?"

"Oh, she's down with what we're going to do," Rufus assured him, but added in his mind, *I hope.*

They placed their right hands in front of themselves, one on top of the other, to signify their determination, and their solidarity.

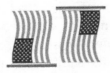

The Golden Springs Town Council invited Roscoe Alolo to speak at its June meeting, on the subject of "Repairing History through Reparations." Dean Meredith Stokes wasn't explicitly invited, but Roscoe assured her that she was welcome, which was good, because she really needed to do something to escape from her current headspace.

In the aftermath of Professor Alolo's courageous letter to the editor of the *Golden Springs Gazette*, the council members — indeed, nearly the entire populace of the town — felt like their eyes had been opened to the subtle menace lurking just upstream on the other side of the gorge. Once Professor Alolo pointed it out to them, they too deplored the repugnant statue standing in central Coon Creek. At the meeting, each member of the council wore a lapel pin with the name "Fink" and a line drawn through it.

At the same time, that scandal led some Golden Springers to wonder if their beloved town's history might not likewise contain hidden violations of political correctness. To their universal chagrin, the council members learned that they had skeletons in their closet, too. Pax Oglesby, who in addition to being facilitator of the common good was also the town's resident historian, discovered several shocking facts. One of Golden Springs's founders, Otto Vine, after whom Vine Street was probably named, disrespected Native American culture by building a hogpen on Shawnee burial grounds. Thaddeus Smock, the second president of Antaeus College, refused to hire female faculty members and was reported to have remarked in private that women should "open their legs and not their books." Even the sainted Johnny Appleseed, who planted an orchard in what was now Amity Valley Memorial Gardens, was rumored to have had a worrisome predilection for little girls. It almost seemed like, in the past, nobody behaved honorably.

After thanking the town council, Professor Alolo spoke: "The ravages of slave labor remain a blight upon the American conscience and is the primary cause of today's economic imbalances and racial strife...."

As stirring as his speech was, it failed to hold Meredith's attention. Under the pretense of taking notes, she re-re-re-read Vanessa's letter, which she'd placed in a pocket of her binder. The letter had arrived via registered mail that morning. Meredith had held it to her breast before reading it. She intuited that it contained bad news, first because Vanessa composed it using a word processor, whereas she'd handwritten every other piece of correspondence she'd sent to her. Furthermore, she had sent it via registered mail, which imbued it with a stark formality. Vanessa would only have done that kind of thing at the advice of a lawyer. The letter began:

I hope this finds you well.

That seemed aloof, yet still positive. The letter continued:

The time has come for us to dissolve our relationship and divide our assets.

She could not envision Vanessa even thinking those words. They sounded like they came from some breaking-up form letter.

> *From the beginning, when you accepted a job in Ohio, I told you that I had reservations about whether we could sustain a relationship via long distance. It is now clear to me that this is not working.*

Meanwhile, Roscoe's speech held the town council in thrall. He spoke with vigor, spitting out vowels as if gargling them and hissing s's to convey a sense of disgust. "Restoring justice must begin with a formal apology from the highest levels of government."

> *I have taken the liberty of removing your name from the lease on my apartment. I have also packed your possessions and shipped them to your address in Golden Springs. If you have any questions or concerns, please address them to my lawyer, whose card is enclosed. I wish you the best. But my mind is made up.*

She signed the letter Sincerely and with her full name, rather than her typical, Love, Nessa.

Meredith slipped the letter out of its binder pocket and held it in both hands, pulling it tight between them, and then slowly, deliberately, ripped it in two. She crumbled the halves into tiny balls. Only then did she realize that people were watching her.

But they quickly returned their attention to Roscoe, who was building to the climax of his oration. "So, yes, my friends, we *must* rend asunder the pages of our biased and erroneous history books. We *must* purge the past. We *must* provide long overdue reparations. That is the least it will take to make things right in America today."

Meredith shouted, "Hear, hear!" and started clapping. Roscoe looked confused, as if he hadn't finished speaking, but the ovation quickly spread across the room. Pretty soon, everybody had stood and started clapping. Roscoe sucked in his gut and took a bow.

Pax Oglesby slammed his gavel and called for order. When the fracas subsided, he spoke. "Those were stirring words, Professor Alolo. I do believe that everybody in our community would benefit from hearing them. So, sir, if you are willing, I would be happy and proud to yield my place to you as the keynote speaker at our Independence Day Festival of Light ceremony. Would you do us the honor of delivering your speech to the entire town?"

"I will do so proudly," Roscoe said. He raised his cane above his head, as if to call down lightning.

While everybody in the room cheered and raised a joyful ruckus, Meredith took advantage of the clamor to mask the sound of her saying "FUCK" out loud. She felt feverish. Spikes of heat burst through the pores across her body. Backing away from the table, she restrained herself until out the door, and then ran as fast as she could down the hall to the women's restroom. She made it to the toilet just in time to vomit green bile.

CHAPTER 11

Toad worried. When she worried, she sweated. When she sweated, she felt sticky, clammy, and stinky. When she felt sticky, clammy, and stinky, she couldn't sleep at night. And when she couldn't sleep at night, she felt down in the dumps. Finally, when she felt down in the dumps, she worried even more about everything and everybody.

In the midafternoon, Toad sat rocking in the shade of her front porch. She drank lemonade by the pitcher and sweated it back out almost as fast. Dixie was sprawled flat on her side, panting. The glare of sunshine rippled off asphalt streets and black shingle rooftops, so that it looked like everything melted upwards. Every so often, a cicada siren loud enough to scare birds out of trees blasted apart the sleepy languor of the day. A mosquito landed on Toad's forearm but didn't bite, it just danced around on her skin for a few seconds, then buzzed away. Was something wrong with her blood?

Zeke was giving Toad plenty to worry about. Over the years, she'd gotten so used to his constant bellyaching about various ailments—from his bunions to bloody stools to hair falling out—that she didn't even hear him anymore. She would always answer, "So go to the doctor already," which he refused to do because he seemed to believe an undiagnosed disease couldn't harm him. Whatever.

Lately, though, Zeke had been having sharp pains in his lower side, which he described as having an ice pick jammed up his asshole. He hardly took a breath that didn't end with "owwww" when he exhaled. Toad knew it must be serious when Zeke consented to see the doctor. As it turned out, he had kidney stones.

But that wasn't what worried Toad the most about Zeke. Having pebbles in a major internal organ wasn't a good thing, but from what she'd read on the internet, they'd squeeze their way out of him, eventually. Worse than that, Toad worried that lately Zeke had been spending nearly every waking moment drinking Iron City beer and whiskey with cranberry juice shots at the Drink Here Tavern. He said that the needed to stay hydrated, but in doing so he was getting pickled. Furthermore, he was paying for his drinks on credit in anticipation of the profits they'd realize when Dixie had her puppies. At the rate he was going, Dixie would have to drop a litter of twenty to pay for all his boozing.

Toad had been so worried and desperate about Zeke's drinking that she sent Boog to try to talk some sense into him. "Won't you please do that much for your mama?" she begged him.

"Roger that," he said to her, which she presumed was military talk for *yes*.

That was a big mistake. Instead of bringing Zeke home, Boog pulled up a stool and drank along with him. Boog had always been a sturdy drinker, able to quaff enormous quantities and still walk a more-or-less straight line. Among the Galoots, that practically qualified him as a teetotaler. So, Toad at least expected Boog to stay sober enough to see that Zeke got home. Instead, she had to fetch Zeke passed out at closing time, while Boog was nowhere to be found.

Toad also worried about Boog. Something had been off about him ever since he got back from Afroganny-stand — Toad could barely name it, much less understand what in the hell a kid from Coon Creek was doing there, fighting a war that nobody knew how or when to end. On the day when Boog came home, Darlene tied a gigantic yellow ribbon around the trunk of the red oak tree in their front yard. His family and friends all turned out to thank him for his service. He let them buy him drinks, and some more drinks. In a matter of weeks, though, he'd exhausted their goodwill. Folks found that just one false word and he would get mad and break something; just mentioning the Cincinnati Reds pissed him off so much he pushed over a pinball machine. As much as Darlene defended him, she, too, became afraid of his temper. Nobody knew exactly what he did to make her finally leave him, but it must've been pretty awful because, on her way out the door, she screamed, "I'll keep praying for you, but so far as I'm concerned, you can rot in hell!"

Toad wiped sweat from her face with a bandana. There may have been a tear or two mixed in with the moisture.

Oh well, she mused, at least Boog had a job, which was more than most of the men in Coon Creek could say. Still, she wasn't wild about his being a "tattoo artist." Back in her day, the only people with tattoos were sailors, bikers, and homosexuals... in various combinations. Now regular people got themselves permanently branded with all sorts of vulgar and freaky designs. Boog himself had a tattoo of an AK-47 on his upper arm; written in blocky letters beneath it was Any Questions?

She didn't know what it meant and was afraid to ask.

Even little Justin, that sweet kid who used to pick dandelion bouquets for his Meemaw, was now fourteen years old and begging Boog to give him his first tattoo. Thank God that Darlene was dead set against it—she insisted that Boog could not put one drop of ink on his body until he turned eighteen. Boog went out of his way to provoke Darlene by saying, "If I did it, it'd be in some place where you'd never see."

On top of all those worries, her most persistent was for Mazie, up there in the urban jungle of Columbus all by herself, beyond her mother's care and protection. The metropolis had been the ruin of many a young person, and Toad could scarcely imagine the kinds of vices and perils present in daily city life. And Mazie didn't always use the common sense she was born with, so she was extra vulnerable. The least she could do was call once in a while, but she was always so freakin' *busy*.

Dixie, lying flat on her side with her tongue hanging out of her mouth, emitted an airy sound that Toad had never heard from her before. It was part whimper, part belch, with a little bit of a sigh mixed in.

"You okay there, Dixie?" Toad asked.

Dixie blinked and lifted her head. Her eyes looked tired and oozed gooey stuff from their corners.

"Poor dear," Toad said. She rocked forward so that she could reach the crop of Dixie's back and began rubbing gently. Dixie wagged her stubby tail to acknowledge the attention, but still seemed woozy.

"I know just how you feel. Morning sickness ain't no picnic," Toad commiserated.

Last but not least of all, Toad worried about Dixie. Her three long walks a day all around the town were down to one to the corner and back in the morning. Toad had a hard time getting her up onto her feet. Just about the only thing that made her happy was going for a car ride. She'd stick her head out the window with her face in the wind, mouth open and ears flapping, and she'd paw at the back of the driver's seat, as if giving directions. She seemed to know where she wanted to go. Toad wished she could talk and tell her what was wrong.

Toad rocked all the way back in her chair and said aloud, "Dang all these problems. It feels like being scared and confused and bothered all at once and in slow motion."

"The whole barn is done painted, Mr. Slocum," Justin reported. "Do yah'll got any more work what I can do?"

Boog Tuttle's kid was so industrious it made Burl tired just keeping him busy. Justin's energy and initiative were commendable, especially given that, in his family, he had only bad examples and dysfunctional role models to guide him. Burl considered himself a positive influence in the kid's life, which was why he didn't want to discourage his ambition. As a purely business proposal, though, their payment arrangement didn't make much sense. Burl's product was worth more on the open market than any amount of unskilled labor that Justin could perform. Boog was getting a great deal and was probably too stupid to realize it.

"I don't know...."

"I could clean out the chicken coop. Ain't done that since last year."

Burl was sitting on a sofa, with his feet propped on a footstool. He pushed aside an empty pizza box and patted the cushion next to him. "Slow down a few ticks, kid."

"I dunno." Justin fidgeted and dug his hands deep into his pockets. "My dad says that if I work more harder, he'll give me a free tattoo."

Burl lifted the top off a cooler on the floor next to him. "Want a beer?"

"Hot dog, I sure do!" Justin blurted out.

Burl pulled a can of beer from the cooler and handed it to Justin, who looked at him and made an *are you sure?* expression before accepting it with both hands. He held it at eye level in front of him, letting cold moisture drip down his hands.

"To open it, pull on that tab," Boog explained, pantomiming to demonstrate the proper method.

Justin cracked the pull tab on the can. He stuck out his tongue and licked around the opening, then tilted the can upside down and gulped three rapid swallows, until the fourth made it just halfway down his throat before getting stuck, reversing course and coming back out of his nose and mouth in an explosive spray.

"Careful, kid. It takes practice to chug a beer."

Justin coughed and coughed, finally catching his breath. "Whoo boy, that's really good," he said.

"You drink your beer like you do everything else, in a hurry."

"I cain't stand still doing nothing, not never."

"Drinking will cure you of that, eventually. Patience comes to those who wait." To demonstrate his point, Burl finished his beer, rubbed his gut, and belched the *ABCs* up to *H*.

"That's freakin' amazing."

"You've got gumption, kid."

"I do? Really? What's that?"

"But it's only useful if you have direction, too. From where I sit, that's what's most lacking in this town. For years and years, folks saw only one direction, the same one that their daddies and granddaddies followed. They griped and groused all the time about their lot in life, but at the same time they were damn proud of who they were and what they did. The path was clear, from cradle to grave, and it defined what it meant to be from Coon Creek. But if you look in just one direction, you have no choice but to follow it, straight over a cliff if that's where it leads."

While Burl spoke, Justin bounced his head often to indicate that he listened — whether he understood was another matter.

"How old are you, kid?"

"Fourteen and a half."

"So that puts you in — what? The eighth grade?"

"Seventh grade. I got held back on account the teacher caught me cheatin'."

"Good for you!" Burl applauded. "Because if you aren't cheating, then you're playing by somebody else's rules. Nobody ever wins by doing that. People think that so long as they play by the rules, they'll be okay. They don't like to rock the boat. The best that can get them, though, is just getting by.

"It's like playing the state lottery. Every week people buy a ticket or two, or however many they need, depending on how desperate they are. Over and over again, they lose. Then every few weeks some lucky son of a bitch wins a huge jackpot, fooling them into thinking, *Next time it could be me*. Somebody's got to win, right? Wrong! Fortunes are made on the wreckage of other people's dreams. The only surefire winners are the ones who rig the system. That is, the cheaters."

Justin's eyelids fluttered.

"Are you paying attention to me!?!"

"Yessir." Justin sprang upright. "You're telling me it's a good thing to cheat."

"Essentially, yes. But there's a difference between cheating and making your own rules. Cheating means manipulating the rules to your advantage. Making your own rules, though, puts you in control. That's crucial because the rules change over time. They always do. People who continue following old rules always lose. I feel sorry for them. I do. But business is business, and doing the 'right' thing is most often bad for business. That's what people in this town just can't get through their thick heads."

"My dad says I got a thick head. But I know this much—just as soon as I turn eighteen years old, I'm getting the hell outta Coon Creek."

"I've heard that story before." Burl chuckled. "You sound just like your Aunt Mazie."

"Mazie? My dad says she's nuttier than a buckeye tree. And more useless."

"For your father to call anybody nuts is like somebody breaking a mirror because they don't like how they look in it. Still, he's sort of right. Mazie couldn't be told anything. If I agreed with her, she'd change her mind just to spite me. We argued about everything. She insisted that she would *break out* of Coon Creek, as if it were the Shawshank Prison. But I said to her that if you can't make it in your own hometown, you won't make it anywhere. Neither of us ever persuaded the other. We just made each other more stubborn.

"In hindsight, I think I did what was right for me. And what she did was right for her. It isn't often that two people get to say 'I told you so' to each other, and both be right."

Burl shifted his feet onto the floor. He rolled his shoulders and lifted his belly, teetering between getting up and remaining seated. This talk teased a memory of a moment with Mazie when he'd either said something or hadn't said it. He reached out with his mind but couldn't bring it into focus. Finally, he sighed and sank back into the chair.

"Can I have another beer?" Justin asked.

Faye prayed. She was quite good at it. Effective prayer was focused, disciplined, and dignified—three values that Faye believed in. The natural dialog of her thoughts was task oriented. She prayed for explanations, not favors. Functional prayer yielded the same catharsis, peace of mind, and sense of transcendence as those berserk evangelicals who spoke in tongues and handled snakes, but without all the absurd excesses.

Normally, Faye could switch from regular thought into prayer mode at will, no matter where she was or what she was doing. If extraordinary circumstances required special or additional prayer, she could step aside, close her eyes, and do a quick check-in with her higher power. Prayer's portability was one of its most useful features.

That morning, though, Faye was so confused and distressed that, try as she might, she could not sustain mindful prayer for more than a few seconds at a time before anxious thoughts and turbulent feelings distracted her. It felt like God was keeping a secret from her. After trying to pray at home, in her lab, and at the cemetery, yet still not feeling any better or even understanding why, she went to the Coon Creek Baptist Church of God to try there.

To her relief, Faye found the church empty. She passed row after row of pews before she slipped into the first. She closed her eyes and cleared out her consciousness. However, her mind refused to still. Against the blackness of her eyelids, she saw flashing colors and brilliant flares, like mental fireworks. She grimaced and squeezed her eyelids tighter until her eyes popped open, as if her eyeballs kicked back suddenly.

Damnit. What was wrong with her? It felt like her brain was turned inside out. She couldn't stop thinking feelings and feeling thoughts.

Faye slid forward in the pew and landed on her knees. The cartilage in her kneecaps crunched. Pain helped her concentrate. Staring into the face of Jesus in a stained-glass window behind the altar, she fought the impulse to blink, as if she was locked into a staring contest with the Lord Almighty. She drew slow, steady, shallow breaths through clenched teeth. Her eyes began to ache. She felt movement in her brain, a synaptic breeze. She felt herself on the brink of an out-of-body experience.

Jesus winked at her.

Faye felt a heavy hand land upon her shoulder. Acting instinctively, she grabbed it and twisted.

"Yeow," Reverend Belvedere squealed. "Uncle!"

After she let go, Faye slapped her own hand for having betrayed her. "I'm sorry, reverend. I just reacted. You startled me."

Reverend Belvedere rubbed his wrist. "I shouldn't have snuck up on you like that. But I was a wee bit worried. You weren't moving. Are you okay?"

Faye straightened her shoulders and tugged on her lapels. She scooched back into a sitting position. "I was praying."

"You seem fidgety."

Faye considered Reverend Belvedere to be an honest man, even a Godly one; but she'd never regarded him as especially perceptive. If he could sense her unease, then it must be obvious. She started to say, *I'm fine*, but when she spoke, she surprised herself by saying, "You're right."

Reverend Belvedere sat down next to her. "If something is bothering you, then you've come to the right place."

"I just... oh, I don't know."

"Here, it doesn't matter what you know. Only what you believe."

"Thank you," Faye said, then wondered — *For what*?

"Belief matters more than knowledge, because when you get right down to it, what does anybody know, really? God works in mysterious ways."

"That's for sure."

"But rest assured that, no matter how unjust or difficult a situation may seem, it nevertheless aligns perfectly with His eternal plan. God is in charge, always."

"I see."

"God tests us. Sometimes, He confounds, frustrates, even aggravates us. When He took my dear Maude from me, I was inconsolable. I could not fathom — *why?* Her death seemed cruel. I wasn't sure that I trusted God."

"Oh?"

"You must know that feeling — don't you? It was a terrible tragedy when your parents died."

Faye bowed her head and gripped the seat beneath her. "Yes, it was."

"But have faith that for every obstacle God places in front of you, He also blesses you with new opportunities. For example, I have found a renewed purpose in running for mayor. The people's support has lifted my heart. Our community is coming together like never before. It's like Mr. Slocum said, 'God gave me the nudge that I needed.'"

"Mr. Slocum? Do you mean Burl?"

"Of course. He loves Coon Creek deeply. I rely upon his counsel. He understands what the people want and need. He has been very encouraging to me."

Were they talking about the same Burl? The Burl Slocum she knew wouldn't encourage another person to breathe unless it served him in some way.

"I'm glad," she said.

"And thank you, too, Faye. When I announced my candidacy, you were among the first people to stand with me."

She wondered if Reverend Belvedere had come up with the idea of running for mayor all by himself, or if Burl had persuaded him. "You're welcome."

"Let's pray together," he suggested. He gave her hand a squeeze. "Lord, Jesus, God Almighty. Let us never forget that You bless us with Your grace at all times, the good and the bad, and even when our troubles seem insurmountable, we trust Your unerring benevolence, for we know that it's through worldly trials that we fortify our souls and prove ourselves worthy of Your love. We must remember that You have a reason for everything that happens. You place hardships upon us because You love us so much."

Reverend Belvedere turned his face to Faye; she'd never noticed before how tiny black pores cratered his nose. He locked into eye contact with her.

"So we must look beyond our petty trials and tribulations. Even in moments when our hearts are heavy, if we seek You through prayer, we will know what to do." Reverend Belvedere placed both hands on Faye's cheeks, held her head steady, and kissed her on the lips.

Faye was too stunned to react. Sexual rigor mortis set in. His dry, cracked lips felt like sandpaper on hers. His breath was steamy and smelled like he'd been chewing on dirty gym socks. Their noses dueled. His hands moved from her cheeks to her shoulders, pulling her close; at first gently, but when she did not move, harder, like trying to pull open a stuck door. He swung one of his legs onto her lap and poked at her hips with a sapling of an erection; it was damp and sticky through his pants. Faye couldn't fight through the shock and disgust to resist. Reverend Belvedere seemed to interpret her passivity as consent. With some fumbling, he managed to loosen her tie and undo the top button of her shirt. His hand was cold when he slipped it under her bra strap.

An intense spasm of nausea liberated her. When he tried to worm his slimy tongue into her mouth, it triggered a gag reflex. Faye heaved violently, as if choking. Simultaneously, she reacted the way she'd been taught to disarm any would-be rapist. She kicked Reverend Belvedere in the nuts.

Reverend Belvedere yipped in pain and groveled on the floor. "Owwwww. Did you have to do that?" he whined.

Faye rose above him, feeling no pity.

"I'm sorry, Faye. I thought we were having a moment," he sobbed.

She toed him in the back.

"Please, please, please. Don't tell anybody about this."

At that instant, Faye's absolute disgust and total revulsion peaked. It wasn't just the reverend — *all men were scum*. Saliva and snot filled her mouth. She gathered the vile juices in her cheeks, swished them around, and then spat right between his eyes.

CHAPTER 12

Roscoe started wearing his Chairman Mao cap again. It was well worn, faded blue, and sweat stained around the headband, but it was still puffy on the top and its visor was sharp. Back in the 1970s, wearing it was a small act of rebellion. Unfortunately, with the only possible exception of El Jefe, none of his summer students understood its erstwhile significance. One of them complimented him for his "beret," as if he were some French peasant instead of a revolutionary.

When he wore the cap in town, though, he received several salutes and thumbs up from passing citizens. These gestures confirmed, to Roscoe's way of thinking, his status as one of Golden Springs's most influential residents and an intellectual trendsetter.

"Thank you, comrade," he said to well-wishers.

After five weeks, the halfway point of the summer residency, Roscoe Alolo felt reborn. He was astonished that things were going so well. The students were compliant but creative, and eager for his mentorship. Antaeus College administration gave him everything he asked for. Whereas he had arrived in Golden Springs worried that time had passed him by, now everybody treated him like a revered elder. Roscoe tried to act nonchalant, as if this was normal for him. Best of all, he was having more fun than at any time since smoking hashish with Snoop Dog on the steps of the Lincoln Memorial during the Million Man March.

On the last session prior to the Independence Day break, Roscoe arrived early for class. This was unprecedented; he had consistently and purposefully arrived late since day one. Half of the students weren't there yet. While waiting, he sat humming "Peace Train" and twirling his cane like a baton. Every time a student entered the room, he made a check mark in his notebook. Mazie was the last to show up.

"We are so honored that you deigned to join us today," he said.

The rubber soles of Professor Alolo's sandals squeaked as he walked from one side of the floor to the other, then back to the podium, where he leaned onto his elbows and spoke: "I've been lying to you. I am not here to teach you to write. You already know that, whether you know it or not. Oh, it's true there are some tricks and techniques I can show you, but nothing you wouldn't eventually figure out for yourselves. Once you've seen one metaphor, you've seen them all. I'm going to share a secret with you. My true job is to teach you to lie.

"Lying isn't as easy as you think. Anybody can speak an untruth. It's as natural as laughing when amused, crying when sad, or screaming when afraid. The only difference is that *any* time is a good time for a lie. Not only will a good lie get you out of a difficult situation, but it can also enhance good times, improve your status, and enable you to win friends and influence people. Ironically, a believable lie strengthens your credibility. Even in the unlikely event you are exposed as a liar, people will still pretend to trust you rather than admit that they were fooled. Once they commit to your lie, they can't turn back.

"Nothing empowers you like getting away with a lie. If you want to succeed as a writer, lie better. Before you tell a lie, think it through completely, with due consideration to time, place, persons, and circumstances, so that your fabrications are rich with detail, intricately complex, and consistent with every retelling. A good lie can be *proven*.

"Fiction lies to you. Poetry tricks you. Even nonfiction deceives you. The relationship between a writer and reader is one of symbiotic fraud. Lies benefit both parties. To a creative writer, the truth is useful only to disguise a lie."

As he spoke, Professor Alolo scanned the room from left to right, from the first row to the last, establishing a moment of visual contact with each person in the class. When he finished, he nodded up and down, as if he had seen what he looked for.

"But you've been lying to me, too, haven't you? You've lied to me about who you are, your expectations, and your motives. You cannot fool a master liar like myself. When you can tell me a lie that I truly believe, that's when you will have earned the right to call yourself a writer."

He held one hand open, upright, and turned toward the class—an invitation, a dare, or a warning; he meant the gesture as all those things.

"For the rest of the day, I want you to work with your groups." He closed his notebook. "Tomorrow, Independence Day, you are free. Do whatever you want. But I encourage you to participate in the festivities sponsored by the community. I'll be the keynote speaker at twilight. I hope to see you there." By which he meant he would check whether or not they came. And that was no lie.

"Are we united?" Taara Ali asked as soon as everybody had settled in their seats.

"Yo," Rufus attested.

"It'll be a blast," Quang said.

"I got nothing better to do," El Jefe concurred.

"Sure," Mazie lied.

At least she thought that she was lying. She hadn't really made up her mind. Part of her believed that the whole half-cocked plan of theirs would only work as a piece of fiction and that they didn't really intend to do it. Another part of her recognized that if they did it they asked for a whole shitload of trouble. Yet another part of her thought it was a dumb idea that might be fun, in the same way that drawing a mustache on the Mona Lisa would be fun.

Mazie snapped out of her train of thought when Professor Alolo's shadow fell upon her.

"Excuse me," he said to all. Then he said to Mazie, "Would you please see me in my office after class, Ms. Tuttle?"

The question initially took her aback. *Well duh,* Mazie thought. Did he forget that he saw her every day after class when she went to take Shabazz for his afternoon walk? Then, noticing the baffled expressions on the faces of her teammates, Mazie realized that the professor made the request for them to see, rather than for her to confirm.

"No problemo," she replied.

Meredith was getting sick and tired of Roscoe Alolo. The more he ingratiated himself with the board of trustees, the town council, and indeed the whole Golden Springs community, the lower her opinion of him sank. He seemed to enjoy their flattery. Vanity was unbecoming of a revolutionary.

She put her disdain of him to good use. Meredith channeled it when she sat down to write her response to Vanessa, summoning a vision of a primping Roscoe Alolo in her thoughts, and that helped to cut through all ambivalence and get right down to feeling bitter and betrayed. If not for keeping the image of Roscoe in her mind, she could never have written the things that she did, much less have mailed that letter, sealed with a loogie. Roscoe was easier to despise than Vanessa, although she deserved it just as much.

Furthermore, Meredith had to begrudgingly acknowledge that her improved status with the board of trustees was a direct consequence of having brought Roscoe onto campus. Pax Oglesby was especially smitten; he referred to Roscoe as "the Guru of Golden Springs." So, despite her exasperation with him, it remained in her best interest to indulge Roscoe, which meant she had to continue bringing him pies.

At first, she resented being Roscoe's personal pie delivery service. Increasingly, apart from the need to placate Roscoe, Meredith was glad for the excuse to get out of town every couple of hours. The drive to Coon Creek was a welcome reality check. Her angst faded almost as soon as Golden Springs vanished in the rearview mirror. The ninety-minute round trip refreshed her more than any session in her two years of cognitive behavioral therapy ever had, and it was free.

On July 3, in anticipation of the holiday, Meredith rationalized that, even though he hadn't specifically asked, Roscoe would surely want to celebrate Independence Day with some extra pie, so she planned a trip to Coon Creek. She took off her shoes when she got in her car and drove barefoot. She rolled down the window and rested her arm on top of the door. She popped in a Dave Matthews Band CD and turned up the volume. Humidity soaked the air and a haze draped the surrounding hills and fields with an airbrushed quality; Meredith felt like she drove into a Monet. When Meredith saw the Good Old Boy Billboard just outside of town — "America is God, guns, apple pie, and the Fourth of July" — she knew that it wasn't intended as funny, but even so she pulled over and cracked up laughing.

A pickup truck slowed down and pulled up beside her. Upon seeing her hunched over in laughter, its driver, a young woman wearing a cowboy hat, called across the cab at her, "Are you okay, ma'am?"

Meredith composed herself and answered, "Yeah." She coughed a couple of times to disguise her laughter.

"Well, have yourself a really good day now."

Even though she'd heard and said "have a good

day" mindlessly a million times, it touched Meredith how sincere it sounded when this cowgirl said it. "Happy trails to you," she replied – she'd always wanted to say that – then continued along her way.

It was midafternoon. Just inside the city limits, Meredith stopped to buy a ten cent cup of lemonade from a little girl with a corner stand. A postman was singing "Zip-a-Dee-Doo-Dah" and skipping along his route. A father and son played catch in the park. A crow landed on top of Philander Fink's coonskin cap and cawed. Meredith took it all in.

There was a parking space right in front of the Hungry Coon Diner. Meredith got out of the car and pushed the door; she was gratified to hear its distinctive squeak. Stopping in the doorway, she called hi to Edith Doody, who waited behind the counter.

"Lookee who's come for pie," Edith said. "It's Meredith from Golden Springs."

Meredith was surprised but pleased that Edith remembered her name. "In the flesh."

"What'll I have yah for?"

Meredith approached the counter and looked at the pie case. "Let me see," she said. "I'll take an apple pie and a cherry pie. Those are essential for the Fourth of July, right?"

"Even in Golden Springs?" Edith asked.

Meredith wasn't sure if that was a serious question or a subtle jibe. She left it alone and continued her visual inventory of the pies. "And I need a key lime pie. Nothing says summer like a key lime pie, am I right?"

"So true."

"And I see you have three pecan pies. Good. I felt guilty the last time, taking the pie from the kind woman."

Meredith smiled, recalling that transaction. "In fact, I'd like to buy one of those extra pecan pies for her. I think she said her name was Faye?"

"Faye Pfeiffer. She eats here often. She's a sweet lady, but kind of strange, what with always wearing those dark suits every day. But I guess that comes with the job when you're a mortician."

Meredith flinched as she absorbed this information, the way a reader might react to an unexpected twist to the plot of a novel. "A mortician," she repeated.

"Yeah. It's funny that you should mention her, because the last time she was here, she asked about you."

"Oh? Why?"

"Just curious I suppose."

"Well, if she asks again, tell her that this pie is compliments of Meredith Stokes."

"Will do. Happy Fourth of July."

"Yes. Happy Fourth of July," Meredith said as she backed out the door with the pies.

While walking around to the driver's seat of her car, Meredith noticed, stapled to a telephone pole, a flyer with a picture of fireworks superimposed on a red, white, and blue background. It read: "Come one. Come all. Food, fun, and fireworks. Coon Creek's all-American Fourth of July Boom-a-Thon. Sponsored by Life Eternal Funeral Services."

Meredith ripped the flyer from the pole, folded it, and tucked it into her purse.

Rufus was hanging out in the alumni house parlor with a copy of *Culture and Anarchy* open on his lap, although he hadn't read a word of it. Shabazz slept at his feet, snoring like a warthog. The door to Professor Alolo's office was closed. Mazie was inside with him.

Lately, when he accompanied Mazie on her evening walks with Shabazz, Rufus sensed that she was finally opening to him, just a crack. When they met, instead of saying "hi," now she asked him "what's up?" and once he learned to expect that greeting, he gave thought to answering in some clever way to break the ice, like:

> *"The international space station," or*
> *"The price of gasoline," or*
> *"A two-letter word indicating direction," or*
> *"My patience."*

There were other potential responses, some risqué ("it's in my pants"), that he had so far refrained from using.

They'd even started teasing and joking around with each other. Once while discussing their favorite hip-hop artists, they decided that their rap names would be "MC Real Money" and "Queen Vanilla Millie," and they both laughed at their private joke. Another night, when Shabazz was in an especially frisky mood and Mazie struggled to hold him back, she handed his leash to Rufus and asked, "Are you man enough to handle this?" Either he read her entirely wrong, or that was flirty. Unfortunately, he was so tongue-tied that not only could he think of nothing to say in return, but he let the leash slip out of his hands and they had to chase Shabazz all the way to Shawnee

Knob. The whole time, Rufus cursed himself for having blown an opportunity. He hoped that he'd get another.

That afternoon, when Professor Alolo interrupted the group and asked Mazie to meet him after class, Rufus didn't know why but he didn't like it, and it disconcerted him even more when Alolo asked her to close the door. Rufus waited outside in agony. Ten minutes. Fifteen minutes. Half an hour. He got up and pressed his ear to the wall, but couldn't hear anything but muted, indecipherable conversation on the other side. For some reason, he couldn't shake the feeling that they talked about him.

Another five minutes passed before the door opened, and when it did nobody came out. Rufus got up and peeked in. He heard the professor say to her: "Trust me."

"Thank you, professor," Mazie said.

Dismissed, Mazie stepped briskly past Rufus on her way out.

"Yo, yo, yo. Maze. What up?"

Mazie kept going, then stopped abruptly, as if relenting to the necessity of speaking to him. "Oh, Rufus," she lamented with a sigh. "Sometimes I think I'm not a good enough liar to be a writer."

"That's Professor Alolo talking, not you."

"No, for once, that's me."

"Do you want to talk about whatever or anything?"

She dropped her shoulders and crossed her arms in front of her chest. "I do. But not now."

"When?"

"Right now, I just want to be left alone to write."

Rufus believed that she wanted to be left alone and that she wanted to write, but not necessarily both at once. In either case, her request left no room for negotiation, so all he could do was let her go and say, "Yo. Okay then."

Shabazz woke up with a snort, clambered to his feet, and went to Mazie, expecting her to pet him, but she walked by him and out the door without pause, leaving it to close by itself. Shabazz whimpered.

Left behind, Rufus and Shabazz looked at each other with blank, lingering eyes, an empathetic exchange between man and dog, both equally clueless.

CHAPTER 13

Faye's feet were getting soaked with dew. A mat of freshly cut grass clumped around her bare heels and between her toes. When she'd gotten dressed that morning, she wondered if it was fashionable to wear socks under her sandals—she honestly had never paid any attention to people wearing sandals. Now, she was glad she'd decided to go sockless. This squishy sensation around the balls of her feet and the ticklishness on her nude arches were new to her.

Walking away from the rising sun, Faye could feel its warmth against the backs of her calves and on the sensitive skin behind the bend of her knee. The cargo shorts that she'd bought from Walmart slipped around her hips, so every few steps she hoisted them and tugged on her belt. It had not occurred to her until she was rummaging through the bargain bins that she didn't know her waist size. She'd never purchased a pair of shorts in her life. They fit fine when she tried them on in the store, but when she took them home and started walking, they sank to her hip bones. She was so annoyed by having to stop and pull them up repeatedly that she untucked her tank top and let its bottom dangle to cover her belt line. It was kind of titillating to wear her shorts so low that they might fall to her feet with any step.

Faye debuted her new look to the dead. She walked her familiar path across the Amity Valley

Memorial Gardens, past the final resting places of friends, neighbors, and family who wouldn't recognize her if they could see her now. She hadn't exposed so much skin since she was a tomboy who went shirtless climbing trees with the boys. In fact, when she'd posed in front of the mirror that morning, she hardly recognized herself. She hadn't realized that her legs were so hairy, and in a sleeveless shirt, the unruly thicket in her armpits looked like a bird's nest in an oak tree hollow. All of her bras looked like flak jackets beneath her tank top, so she wore none. She thought of her new look as unkempt chic. It felt liberating.

Same as every morning, she got up at the crack of dawn to raise the American flag. Same as every Fourth of July, the particular flag that she ran up the pole was a family heirloom, for it had once flown above the Capitol Building in Washington, DC. Again, same as every Fourth of July, she attached the flag of the state of Ohio to wave beneath Old Glory. But unlike any Fourth of July, or ever in her life, she also raised a third flag below the others, a brand new flag that had never flown anywhere in Coon Creek, but which, she hoped, reflected and complemented her change of attitude. After securing all three flags aloft, Faye saluted them.

A string of firecrackers blasted a reveille that abruptly fractured the morning calm. Faye covered her ears. The good old boys were getting an early start this year. It would probably get a lot louder before the end of the day.

The labyrinth in the Peace Park of Golden Springs was modelled after the one in the cathedral at Chartres. A local sculptor had assembled it with black rocks, river-polished pebbles, multicolored crystals, and geode halves. According to the bound ledger in the weatherproof box at the labyrinth's entrance, pilgrims had come from spiritual communities as far away as Findhorn, Christiania, Tamera, Auroville, Ananda in Assisi, and the Finca Bellavista treehouse community of Costa Rica to walk its circuits. On every American national holiday, as well as Earth Day, May Day, Darwin Day, International Friendship Day, World Oceans Day, Pi Day, Johnny Appleseed Day, May the Fourth (Be With You), and other minor feasts, including birthdays and bar mitzvahs, one or another of Golden Springs's civic groups sponsored a walk-thru of the labyrinth. However, in recognition of "life, liberty, and the pursuit of happiness," the Fourth of July was the labyrinth's biggest annual event.

Standing at the entrance to the labyrinth, Pax Oglesby addressed the long line of perambulators: "Welcome to our community. We're all friends here today. We come from near and far to gather at the spiritual center of our community, to celebrate the birth of an idea — that all people are free and equal, with the right to live as they please and to be true to themselves in the manner envisioned by this nation's Founding Fathers, and also its overlooked Founding Mothers, Founding Sexual Minorities, Founding Persons of Color, and those Founders with Special Needs. It's about time they all got some of the love, gratitude, and recognition they deserve, too."

Cheers, shouts, and whistles erupted from the crowd. Pax allowed the ovation to die down before continuing. "Today, we are honored to have Doctor Roscoe Alolo—a tireless crusader for truth and justice—as our grand marshal."

Roscoe tipped his Mao cap and flashed a peace sign. "Unity!" he declared, triggering a chant of "Unite! Unite! Unite!"

Roscoe led the queue of walkers on their circuitous stroll. Person after person shuffled along, taking slow, cleansing breaths with each step. There were so many pilgrims that some finished when others were just starting, and the people in this unbroken procession inched along at a synchronized pace, careful not to inadvertently step on toes, shoelaces, or any sentient creature. Within the sphere of the labyrinth, all adhered to strict silence and flowed as one, in hushed deference to their collective consciousness. Upon completing the journey, though, some wept, some whooped, some beat their chests, and others shouted joyous exclamations straight from the depths of their purified souls. Those who had finished gathered around a table where they refreshed themselves with fresh fruit, vegan pastries, and Darjeeling tea. Vendors sold commemorative T-shirts, refrigerator magnets, and bumper stickers that proclaimed, "I walked the Golden Springs Labyrinth."

At once, a deafening explosion thundered through the air. People scrambled to escape, ducked for cover, or hid behind any solid object, including each other. When a second bomb went off, panic set in. People ran in all directions.

"Remain calm," Roscoe pleaded. "It's only a firecracker."

But in Golden Springs, where pyrotechnics had been banned since the twentieth century, nobody had ever heard a firecracker, so a cherry bomb might as well have been a hydrogen bomb.

"Who dares to sully our holiday with such a terrible thing?" Pax Oglesby asked the sky.

His answer came in the form of bottle rocket whizzing so close as to part his hair.

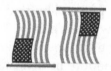

Toad tried to reassure the terrified dog by talking baby talk. "It's okeydokey, Dixie Wixie."

Thwarting her efforts, another ballistic firecracker detonated nearby. It sounded like it came from the alley behind Joe's Sunoco. Everybody, including local law enforcement, knew that Joe made annual excursions to the Indian reservation in Michigan to acquire his arsenal. So long as he reserved the munitions for use only on the Fourth of July, New Year's Eve, and Ohio State University football victories, nobody complained. A lot of people around Coon Creek considered his artillery a community resource. Although it rattled her ears something awful, Toad was loath to ruin everybody else's fun by making a fuss.

But she was incensed on Dixie's behalf. "Those fiddle-faddle fireworks are janglin' poor Dixie's wits," she complained to Boog.

Beer in hand, Boog drawled, "Awww, for shit's sake, Ma. It's all in good fun."

"Fun! That's easy for you to say. You ain't a pregnant dog with very sensitive ears."

"It's just for one day. She'll get used to it, same as I did in Afghanistan. Fireworks clear the head. They're patriotic."

"Baloney! They just make noise. Ain't no more patriotic than yakking out loud."

"Not so," Boog differed and then belched a perfect yak out loud.

Justin entered the room and said, "It's right there in the 'Star-Spangled Banner,' Meemaw." He started singing in a cracking adolescent voice.

> *And the rocket's red glare*
> *The bombs bursting in air*
> *Gave truth... la, la, la*
> *That our flag was still there.*

Toad went "pffft" and returned to comforting her dog. "Here's your blanket, Dixie. I'm a-gonna wrap it all around you like this." She tucked the blanket under Dixie's haunches and forelegs. Dixie let her do it without moving.

Boog's patience vanished with the last gulp of his beer. "C'mon, boy," he said to Justin. "We don't wanna be late for the start of the parade."

"Yeah, yeah, yeah. You're coming, too, ain't you Meemaw?"

Toad wasn't sure how to answer that question. Missing a Fourth of July parade was unthinkable and downright unpatriotic. It would pain her to leave Dixie behind in such fear and dismay, though. Buying time, Toad turned away from Boog and Justin and looked down the hallway beyond them.

"Where's Zeke?" she asked.

Boog answered, "He's been in the toilet ever since me 'n' Justin got here. I think he's constipated."

Toad knew that Zeke was never constipated, and especially not since he'd been drinking gallons of beer and cranberry juice cocktails every day.

"I'd better go check on him," she said.

Zeke rarely closed the bathroom door. Generally, he had no qualms about moving his bowels with the door wide open for anybody to see, hear, and smell. Toad thought he took pride in it. Under other circumstances, she would've walked right in. Something told her that she had better knock first, though.

"What're you doing in there?" she asked, then added for levity, "Writing a book?"

"Eeeeeooooowwwww!!!!!" Zeke croaked.

Toad opened the door a crack and peeped in. Zeke sat on the toilet, pants at his ankles, while cupping his dick and balls in both hands.

"It huuuuurrrrrttttts, Toad. I feel like I'm pissin' out the fuckin' Rock of Gibraltar instead of some dang kidney stone."

Zeke looked pathetic with his eyes smeared with tears and snot, his face flushed pink, and his chin hanging like dead weight.

"Do you want that I should call the doctor?" she asked.

Zeke squeezed his package, bawled, and ground his teeth. "That damn quack'll just tell me to drink more juice." There was a thirty-two-ounce Big Gulp full of cranberry juice cocktail on top of the toilet tank.

"Well, drink up then."

Zeke complained, "If I drink any more of that stuff, my nuts will turn into cranberries."

Toad wished she had some helpful advice to give him, but Zeke was very sensitive about any problem that involved his manhood and not likely to listen, anyway.

"I'm going to the parade with Boog and Justin," she informed him. "I'll check up on you when I get back."

"Eeeeeooooowwwww!"

Toad thought, *If he thinks that hurts, he should try having a baby.* She had a lot more sympathy for Dixie than she did for him.

Nobody could pinpoint the source of the unlawful, inconsiderate, and potentially lethal fireworks that had broken out like a plague in Golden Springs. Whoever was responsible kept on the move. People sought shelter. Citizen guardians patrolled the streets, armed with notepads to record any suspicious activity, or to issue citations if they caught the culprits in the act. They aimed to make the streets safe in time for the parade.

The din was especially turbulent on the Antaeus College campus.

"It is a celebration of war," Taara Ali griped. "Very much like Americans—loud and bossy, not caring what anybody else thinks."

"It makes them happy," Quang said.

And El Jefe added, "They're happy assholes."

"Back in the hood of East Cleveland, people were relieved if the bangs and booms were *only* firecrackers," Rufus said.

Apart from the effect the noise had on Shabazz, Mazie really didn't mind it too much. The blasts distracted her from thinking about things she didn't want to think about. Poor Shabazz, though, was spooked and had been hiding under the chessboard table in the alumni house parlor ever since the first explosion.

Mazie tried to console him with a beef jerky. "Here you go, buddy." When Shabazz sniffed but refused to take it, she knew he was seriously terrified.

Rufus bent down next to Mazie and reached under the table to rub Shabazz behind the ears. While continuing to pet the dog, he said to Mazie, "It's almost time for the parade to start. We have to go now if we don't want to miss it."

"I can't wait to see Professor Alolo on his float," Quang said. "He brought Hershey's Kisses to throw to people."

Mazie kind of wanted to see that, too. But she felt guilty leaving the dog alone. Together with Rufus, she caressed Shabazz, as if apologizing for abandoning him.

El Jefe said, "I'm not afraid of any puny fireworks," and left.

Taara tsked and went with him, followed by Quang, who shouted, "Wait for me."

Rufus and Mazie looked at each other, then at Shabazz, before getting up and jogging to catch up with the others.

The Coon Creek Grand Old USA Independence Day Parade was a passionate display of patriotism and a rip-roaring blowout of a good time that did America proud. Boog wore his T-shirt with Born Free on the front and USA on the back as his small contribution to honoring America. He met the Galoots, just back from raising a little hell in Golden Springs, as the parade got started.

"How'd it go?" he inquired.

"Them hippies covered their heads like the sky was falling," Tank bragged.

Boog had reserved a prime viewing location by cordoning off a section of the sidewalk in front of the Belvedere for Mayor Headquarters with police tape. He had lugged a cooler to the spot; it was full of enough beer to tide the Galoots over until the Drink Here Tavern opened.

His mother didn't approve; she took one look and volunteered to take Justin "to a better spot," although Boog clearly understood her to mean that she wished to shield the boy from the drinking and carousing he intended to do.

"Yah'll git along with your Meemaw," Boog said.

"But Paw, you promised...."

"Not now. Later."

Obedient if not appeased, Justin let Toad lead him to another block, where a clown made balloon animals. Justin asked for a crawdad.

Boog never missed the Fourth of July parade, and every year he remarked it was just as good as the last year. That's because the parade was almost identical from year to year. In fact, that's what he liked about it. Familiarity, consistency, regularity—all in all, it was what folks in Coon Creek called "tradition." In good times, the parade celebrated success, and in bad times it provided diversion. Tradition absorbed every contingency through the filter of selective memory.

The parade began, of course, with the Coon Creek High School marching band. They played "25 or 6 to 4" so loud and fast that it sounded like an alarm clock on amphetamines. Boog sort of sang along, and when he didn't know the words he belted out:

> Ba da ba da bum
> Ba da ba da bum
> Ba da da da da da da bum

The band major was a cute girl whose costume was tight and glittery; she kept dropping the baton, but every time she did, she got a sympathetic ovation.

Next came the classic cars, each one an American-made gas-guzzler. None of them were in what you might call mint condition—some seemed held together with superglue—but they were all clean, down to the gleaming grilles and shiny tires. Paddy drove the same 1960 Corvair that his father had told him he'd been born in. The slow rolling motorcade included several extinct models: Packards, LaSalles, DeSotos, Studebakers, and even a Tucker 1948 sedan. Their bygone era was before Boog's time, but even so he felt a weird nostalgia for them, like a déjà vu for something that had never happened. Coon Creek was a lot like those old automobiles—obsolete, beat up, but still running.

The town's one and only firetruck followed the cars, washed and waxed for the day, and accompanied on foot by members of the volunteer fire department sweating in their slickers and helmets, each one carrying a boot and soliciting spare change to support the cause. It'd been a bad year for fires, and they looked tired. When he got back from Afghanistan, Boog wanted to join them, but somebody mentioned urine tests, and that discouraged him from trying. Not one to hold a grudge, though, he put a dollar in a boot when they marched by.

Then came the floats, Boog's favorite part. Joe of Joe's Sunoco led the way as usual, driving his hook-and-chain wrecker, draped with red, white, and blue streamers, with its windows wide open and its sound system blaring a continuous loop of "Ragged Old Flag," "American Soldier," "Some Gave All," "Where the Stars and Stripes and the Eagle Fly," and "God Bless the USA." Missing that year was "Born in the USA," which Max used to like until he read the lyrics. Ms. Nixon's middle school class contributed its usual oversize American flag made entirely of Lego blocks. The women of the public library's book club dressed as Washington, Jefferson, Franklin, and Lincoln, and sat around an overturned barrel on a flatbed trailer, passing a paper and scribbling on it to simulate the signing of the Declaration of Independence. The Coon Creek Diner sponsored a float with a giant cherry pie made of crepe paper, chicken wire, and tennis balls spray-painted red, pulled by a milk truck. The Drink Here Tavern's float featured Buzz wearing an Uncle Sam costume complete with a top hat and billy-goat beard; he sat on a stool in front of a bar, raising a glass of beer to toast Old Glory.

Annually, the AMVETS sponsored the last float, which they dedicated to America's warriors. On it, actual veterans of World War II reenacted the flag raising at Iwo Jima. Owing to their age and fragility, though, the men were seated, and the flag was borne by bungee cords. Usually Faye Pfeiffer walked alongside the float and handed out peppermint candies and miniature copies of the US Constitution, but this year she was strangely absent. Boog was disappointed because he'd misplaced the copy he'd picked up last year, and this year he intended to actually read it to see what it said about the right to bear arms.

Finally—and anticlimactically as far as Boog was concerned—Very Important Persons rode by in convertibles to schmooze and be seen. Mayor Ball received jeers and cheers in nearly equal amounts, all the while keeping the same fake smile frozen on his face. The Coon Queen hugged a bouquet of roses and blew kisses to admirers. Burl Slocum drove a tractor bearing a giant Reverend Belvedere for Mayor sign, and he was followed, on horseback, by the reverend himself, wearing American-flag and Jesus-fish lapel pins, and a Make American Great Again baseball cap, while tossing fun-size candy bars from his saddle bag. To show his approval, Boog saluted him with one of his famous two-fingered whistles.

After the parade was over and most of the crowd had dispersed, Boog and the Galoots reconvened at their corner, finishing the last of the beers in the cooler to lighten it before they proceeded to their next destination. Toad returned with Justin and asked Boog if he minded that she took him to the Coon Creek Baptist Church of God's ice cream social for a treat.

"Sure," Boog replied. "Just make sure to have him back by dinnertime."

"Of course," Toad agreed, then asked, "Will I see you at the fireworks this evening?"

Boog looked down and shook his head sideways. "I don't think so, Maw. We got something special planned."

Boog was relieved that she didn't press for details. If she knew, she wouldn't approve.

Marveling at the sight, Mazie sputtered, "Whoa. This is so... I don't know. It's sure different from the Fourth of July parade where I come from."

"How so?" Rufus asked.

Without thinking it through, she replied, "It isn't white trash."

"Huh? White trash? You're from New Albany, right?"

Damn, she caught herself telling the truth again. Ever since Professor Alolo called her bluff, she feared she was losing her touch. She sometimes forgot who she was lying to, and why.

"I just meant that it's different here. I mean, like, look at it...."

The Golden Springs Peace and Love Parade had no clear beginning or end. Anybody who felt so inspired was welcome to step off the curb and become part of the fanfare. The Team of Strangers had come to watch it together, but quickly separated into other pursuits. Quang got into the spirit right away, joining a gang of undergraduates tossing Frisbees and doing trick catches. El Jefe accepted a joint passed to him and fell in with the cannabis-rights crowd, who chanted: "Stop the lies! Legalize!" When Taara Ali saw a bunch of white ladies from a belly-dancing class moving and shaking in the streets, she called out, "Cultural appropriation!" and, knotting together the loose ends of her shirt, jumped in to show them the proper method.

Mazie felt like an anthropologist doing fieldwork. She locked her arm around a lamppost so she could watch without getting swept into the fracas. She appreciated Rufus for staying with her, to serve as a second set of eyes to confirm what she saw.

It was more of a mob party than a parade. Instead of a marching band, there were buskers, wandering minstrels, bongo drummers, a barbershop quartet, and bagpipers. Square dancers do-si-doed in the fire lane and swung unwitting partners who just happened to pass by. A lawn mower drill team executed complex maneuvers in the street. Dominatrixes in leather led middle-aged men wearing diapers on studded leashes. Zombies and mermaids walked arm in arm. Mazie had to do a double take before she realized that the body-painted people riding unicycles were, in fact, totally nude.

"Did you see that?" Mazie asked Rufus.

"Butts, boobs, and dicks," Rufus replied.

Mazie simultaneously thought, *That's so cool*, and, *I could never do that.*

They commented on every float that went by them. Mazie noted that the queen bee on the Save the Bees float was a man in drag. Rufus wondered what, exactly, was the point of Mother Earth and the Grim Reaper riding on the same float. When women tossed condoms from the Planned Parenthood float, Mazie caught one and put it in her purse. She and Rufus both agreed that the six-foot-tall vagina riding a motorcycle was way over the top.

At the finale of the parade, the master of ceremonies, Roscoe Alolo, rode by in a float decorated in Ndebele patterns. Instead of his Mao cap, he wore a kufi hat. A spear-wielding crew of Zulu warriors marched alongside him. The crowd loved it. They chanted "A-lo-lo, A-lo-lo." Periodically, the float stopped and, from his pedestal, Roscoe declaimed, "*Dawa ya moto ni moto.*"

Everybody cheered as if they knew what that meant.

The parade continued long after it ended. Since its momentum was going in their direction, Mazie and Rufus fell in behind a group of rodeo clowns playing kazoos, which they followed to the edge of town. There, the parade turned back on itself and returned in the direction from whence it had come. Suddenly alone, Mazie and Rufus doubled over with laughter, as if until that moment they had been struggling to keep straight faces.

"Un-fucking believable," Mazie said when she finally recovered control of her diaphragm.

"Yeah, but so real," Rufus said.

They continued sporadically giggling as they walked back to the Antaeus College campus, although the more distance they put between themselves and the melee in town, the more their silliness dissipated. Mazie began to feel awkward, in a way that reminded her of waking up next to somebody after a one-night stand. Rufus was breathing through his teeth; he seemed to desperately want to say something.

Mazie thought she knew what it was. "About tonight...." she said.

"Yeah. I was thinking about that." Rufus turned, and they were standing face to face. "Are you in?" he asked.

"I think so. Maybe. I haven't decided."

Rufus nodded. "I get it."

"Really? Because I don't get it."

"Oh, I do. Really, I do," he assured her.

He doesn't get it, Mazie thought.

She was about to tell him to forget that she'd ever mentioned it, but when she hesitated, Rufus answered the question she really wanted to ask.

"Whatever you decide to do, it's all good," he said.

He squeezed her hand, and she squeezed back.

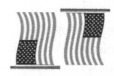

Meredith did not want to walk the labyrinth and was in no mood to participate in that Woodstock reenactment Golden Springs called a parade. She didn't feel like doing anything, but needed to do something, because doing nothing made her antsy. Of course, she had Vanessa at the forefront of her mind—how she felt hurt, angry, rejected, betrayed—but her feelings expressed themselves in just one word: so. So what? So what went wrong? So what was she supposed to do? So what was she supposed to feel? So... just so. There were no obvious answers to any of her *so*'s.

Meredith sat at her kitchen table in front of a plate of pecan pie and her third glass of Ohio River Valley Pinot Gris. She figured that drinking and eating were two time-tested methods for dealing with a breakup. But she didn't feel heartbroken, exactly. Not heartsick, either. Instead, Meredith felt heart empty. Void. Numb. Hollow inside and dead outside. The alcohol wasn't providing relief from her symptoms. The more she drank, the more it drained her.

A firecracker going off somewhere nearby made her jump. She felt her heart beat furiously, from her fingertips to her temples. The sound shook her head enough to temporarily distract her from self-pity. Then it hit her: that's what she wanted to do—blow something up. She wanted to surround herself with deafening blasts of munitions, feel the backlash of their explosions, see pyrotechnic flames combusting all around her. Burn, baby burn.

And she knew just where to go to experience those things. Pulling on a pair of jeans and a tiger-striped Cincinnati Bengals T-shirt that she'd bought for a Halloween costume, she grabbed her keys and the bottle, and drove to Coon Creek to see the Boom-a-Thon.

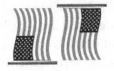

It was late afternoon by the time Toad got home. She'd enjoyed the ice cream with Justin, even though hers melted before she could finish it. Justin said a beer ice cream float sounded good, and when Toad asked him how he knew, he sputtered, "I mean *root* beer." She let it drop. The boy was clearly excited by "the plans" that his father had for that evening, whatever they were; he gave no details other than to say that "it'll be the bomb." Toad didn't know if she should take that remark literally. She hoped there wouldn't be actual bombs.

After dropping off Justin, Toad mingled for a while with friends around the town square, where the statue of Philander Fink wore an American flag draped over its shoulders. Folks gathered there for a picnic and free bluegrass concert at the gazebo. The band never showed up, so eventually folks started singing and dancing on their own. Toad sang along with everybody on an a capella version of "Wabash Cannonball." Those with food shared it with those who had none. Toad wasn't even a little bit hungry, but even so ate a hot dog and some deviled eggs. She lost a game of cornhole to Edith Doody, but won the rematch; they didn't keep score for the rubber game.

Toad would have been content to stay there the rest of the day, but she worried about Dixie. The poor dog hadn't been outside all day, and Toad assumed it was the same with a dog as with a woman — when you're pregnant, you have to piss a lot. Poor dog. Thinking about Dixie hiding and trembling in the laundry room made Toad feel guilty about having so much fun. She went home to check in on her.

"Dixie!" she called out when she came through the door. "I'm home, girl."

The only response she got was Zeke grunting softly.

Ignoring him, Toad called a second time, "Dixie. Come, Dixie."

"Ooooohhhhhooooowwwww," Zeke sobbed. "Damnit, Toad. Leave the dog be. I'm hurtin' something awful."

Toad found Zeke sprawled on the sofa, his robe open at the front, with a tray of ice cubes on his genitals.

"I done passed my stone," he announced.

"Where's Dixie?" was all that Toad cared to know.

"Look here." He held up his thumb and index finger, pinching a tiny mote smaller than a grain of salt between them. "It felt like a chain saw coming out."

Toad refused to look at anything that had passed through Zeke's urethra. "Where's Dixie?" she repeated.

Zeke blew the mote off his fingers. "She ain't here," he said. "Somebody lit up a firecracker in an empty garbage can, and it sounded like a stick of dynamite. It spooked the dog something awful. She pawed the back door open and dashed away."

"What? Zeke, how could you just let her run off like that?"

"I cain't hardly move."

"Where to did she go?"

"How ought I to know?"

Toad huffed and informed Zeke that he was a useless turd, then left in search of her dog.

For the next few hours, Toad looked high and low, all over town. She combed Coon Creek from the welcome sign on Main Street, up and down the numbered streets, to the alleys and back streets. She looked in the trailer park and where they dumped their trash. She circumnavigated the old Hercules Mill three times, calling for Dixie over and over. She sniffed the bushes where Dixie usually pissed, trying to catch a scent. She peeked into vacant houses and boarded up storefronts and looked in dumpsters. She traversed the paths in the Amity Valley Memorial Gardens and looked down into open graves. Lastly, she walked the grounds of the high school stadium, where folks were already laying blankets to secure their spots for viewing the fireworks. Everybody that she asked said they hadn't seen Dixie but wished Toad luck finding her.

Toad saw a strange woman working in the cordoned-off blast zone, loading shells into cylinders on the launchpad. When she called "hey," the woman turned, and Toad did a double take when she realized the woman was Faye Pfeiffer, looking like she'd just been released from a women's prison.

"Faye?"

"Oh, hello Gertrude," Faye replied nonchalantly. "It's going to be a great show tonight."

"I'm sure it will be. But, Faye, have you seen Dixie?"

"No, sorry."

By then, Toad had exhausted every possible hiding place she could think of within the Coon Creek metropolitan area. She sat down on a curb and scratched her head. At a loss, Toad asked herself, *If I were a scared dog, where would I go?*

Toad weighed the facts. Evidently, Dixie had left Coon Creek, so she needed to look farther afield. The quickest way out of town was around the stadium, beyond the fence line, and to cut through the farmers' fields to the state highway. She thrashed through uncut hay and dodged gopher holes as she tromped along, calling "Oh Dixie, Hey Dixie, Dixie Girl" nonstop, like an auctioneer. At length, she emerged from the brush and onto Route 343, at the point where the road turned to face the giant billboard on the outskirts of town.

A truck approached. Toad flagged it down by waving her arms like a windmill. "What's going on?" Burl Slocum asked her when he pulled over and rolled down the window.

"Dixie!" Toad panted. "Have you seen my dog?"

Burl jawed on that question for a few seconds, then answered, "I think maybe I might have. A dog that looked a lot like her was roaming that old dirt road just beyond the steel bridge, on toward the hills."

"That's it! I know where she's going," Toad cried to Burl. "Can you take me there?"

"Wait a minute there, Toad. I was just on my way into town to see the fireworks."

Toad burst into a deluge of tears. She sank to her knees, blubbering. "Please, I'm begging you."

"Stop that. I cain't stand to see a woman cry." Burl squeezed his fingers into the notches on the steering wheel. "Oh, what the hell. Get in. Let's see if we can find that mutt of yours."

"Glory will be ours," Taara said, heaving the hooks and ropes into the back of El Jefe's van.

"It'll be fun," Quang added.

"It's also illegal," Rufus pointed out.

"No, it is civil disobedience," Taara corrected him, unwrapping her hijab and stuffing all her hair into a baseball cap that could barely contain it all. "That is what makes it glorious."

"It wouldn't be as much fun if it was legal," Quang said.

El Jefe checked the list to confirm they had everything they needed, then slammed shut the hatch on the van. He checked his watch. "Where's your girlfriend, Rufus?"

"Mazie is not my girlfriend," Rufus asserted, although El Jefe thinking so pleased him. "She should be back from walking Shabazz by now. Maybe I should go look for her."

"No," Taara said. "She knows the plan. If she is not here in ten minutes, we will have to leave without her."

"She'll be here," Rufus stood up for her, even though he was not at all sure of her intentions.

Quang said, "We might as well listen to some tunes while we're waiting. He turned up the volume on his Bluetooth speaker; "American Idiot" started streaming. The song moved him to embark upon a spastic air guitar solo. He lip-synched, thrashed his imaginary instrument, and strutted around in a Jaggeresque manner, urging the others to join him. Taara huffed and turned her back, but after a while she peeked over her shoulder at him, and with a faint smile on her face, began strumming an invisible bass. El Jefe tapped his foot and started drumming on the hood of his van. They looked unworried about the felony act of terrorism they were about to commit. Rufus didn't share their smugness.

Walking around the van, Rufus stopped behind a maple tree to take a piss. Nothing was coming out. It felt like someone was watching him. Peering around the side of the tree, he saw his teammates; they were too busy acting like fools to notice him. Then he looked up, where from a branch just above his head, two beady raccoon eyes gazed down upon him.

"Help," he heard Mazie's voice carry over the music. She ran toward them, arms and legs flailing, hair flying everywhere.

Rufus hurried to meet her. She bent over, hands on knees, panting. "Shabazz," she said.

"Shabazz? What about Shabazz?" Rufus asked.

"He's gone." Mazie righted herself and caught her breath. "When I went to take him on his afternoon walk, he was missing. He'd clawed through the screen door, probably scared by the firecrackers."

El Jefe reassured her, "It's nothing. Loud noises make dogs panic. He will hide until they are done, and then go back home. You'll see."

"No. I'm responsible for him. There will be hell to pay if something happens to him."

"We have to leave now," Taara said.

"I can't," Mazie said. "I just can't."

"Come on," Quang urged her. "You don't want to miss this."

"I can't," Mazie said again. She stood up straight, as if behind a line drawn in the dirt.

Rufus took a step onto her side. "I'll help you look," he said.

Taara kicked the ground and shook her shoulders so hard that the baseball cap flew off her head, and her mane of kinky hair sprang loose. "No, no, no, no, no. You cannot back out now. We need both of you to do this."

"Naw, we don't really," Quang disagreed. "Fuck 'em if they don't want to join the party."

El Jefe started the van and Quang hopped into the seat next to him. Before she got in, Taara spoke: "You are no longer part of our team."

Mazie and Rufus watched the Team of Strangers drive away for their date with destiny. "We might regret this," Rufus said.

"Not me." Mazie sounded certain.

Rufus only had to think for a second before he said, "I think I know where Shabazz went."

"Really. Let's go. Where?"

Rufus pointed toward the darkening woods. Mazie nodded that she understood. The grateful expression on her face removed any doubt Rufus had about his decision. *Fuck making a moral statement*, he thought. *I've got a date.*

Tank couldn't resist lighting a cherry bomb and tossing it into a culvert. When it blew, thunder resounded out of both ends, like an explosion in surround sound. People sitting in the fairway ducked and covered their heads with their arms. Tank chortled in delight.

Boog was not amused; he grabbed Tank by the collar and snarled "asshole" in his face.

"Aw, shit on fire, Boog. I'm just having me a little fun."

"Your fun is gonna give away our location," Boog rebuked him. "And ruin the element of surprise."

The town of Golden Springs prided itself on its expansive, multiuse green spaces. Among the most prized tracts of undeveloped land was a five-mile-long strip alongside Elixir Creek, which was named the "Boulevard of Verdant Dreams." In addition to providing townsfolk with paths for walking and biking, a fitness trail, a safe playground, an outdoor amphitheater, and a chanoyu tea house, there was a world-class Frisbee golf course, where the spacious grounds around the eighteenth hole and clubhouse provided a perfect viewpoint and launch pad for the town's Fourth of July festivities.

The Galoots were hiding on a little knoll in a copse of lilac trees overlooking the eighteenth fairway. Boog trained his binoculars at the clubhouse patio. It felt like being back in Kandahar, scoping out the enemy.

A string quartet was playing some la-de-da music that sounded like something he might hear in a dentist's office to calm a person facing a painful procedure. Surrounding the stage were hundreds of people preparing their luminaries for ignition and liftoff. Inconceivably, nobody was drunk or even a tad disorderly — Boog wondered what was wrong with these people; they looked to him like congregants in some kind of weird liberal cult, ready to drink the Kool-Aid. He almost felt sorry for them.

Boog lowered his binoculars and asked, "Are you ready, boy?"

Justin was tying his sneakers. "Yeah, yeah, yeah. Can I go already?"

"Let's go over the plan once more. You gotta act like you belong here. Right?"

"Can I have a beer, Daddy? That'll make me calm."

Buzz didn't wait for Boog to answer the boy. He cracked open a can of Blatz and handed it to him. When Boog scowled at him, Buzz grinned and said, "He's doing a man's job. He deserves a man's drink."

"Just one," Boog said, then continued strategizing. "So, you'll walk through the rough, keeping your distance, but not so much that you attract attention. If somebody looks at you, wave like you're just another idiot. Walk around to the side of the clubhouse. There are three little steps onto the patio. You have to make sure you've got a clear path, all the way to the speaker's podium. As soon as that asshole gets ready to talk, I'll light off an M-80. When you hear it, run as fast as you can, and don't slow down. Do it, then skedaddle off the other side of the patio, behind the clubhouse, through the pines, around the duck pond, and meet up with Paddy, who'll wait for you in the pickup on the other side. Meanwhile, we'll rain down a whole javelin missile's worth of fireworks, to let them know what a real honest-to-goodness American Fourth of July is supposed to sound like. Kaboom. That's the sound of freedom, boy."

"Yeah, yeah. Sure, sure," Justin cut him off. "And after that you're going to give me my first tattoo, just like you promised."

"If that's what you want, son. You'll have earned the right."

"Oh, I want it, alright. On my butt, where Momma will never see, a great big pair of lips, so I can tell everybody to kiss my ass."

Boog teared up. "That's my boy."

Meredith had never experienced a homespun, small-town Fourth of July; it felt to her like being an extra in an episode of *The Andy Griffith Show*. The whole town had turned out to frolic and cut loose, and for that one day in the middle of the summer, incited by patriotic fervor, neighborly goodwill, booze and junk food, Coon Creek was an idyllic place.

She found a parking spot just large enough for a miniature pony, perfect for her Smart car, right up front near the stage and adjacent blast zone, close enough so that she could've tossed a ping-pong ball into one of the mortar tubes. She walked in circles through the crowd, going nowhere, brushing shoulders and offering a cheery "hiya" to everybody she passed. While waiting in line to buy a sno-cone, she chatted with an elderly couple, who told her they hadn't missed a single Boom-a-Thon in their forty years of marriage. When she couldn't decide on what flavor of sno-cone she wanted, the stringy-haired teenager at the booth suggested that she try "dragon fruit," because even though its name sounded like something awful, everybody who tried it liked it. Dogs played off leash. A boy was carrying his girlfriend piggyback. A speaker on the stage encouraged people to purchase raffle tickets by promising them a chance at winning a freezer. Meredith sucked on her sno-cone, and when an oldies band took the stage and started playing "Pour Some Sugar on Me," she surprised herself by letting out a whoop, which earned her a tip of the beer bottle from an old-timer sitting on a lawn chair nearby.

What's gotten into me? Meredith wondered. Whatever it was, it felt right.

Meredith leaned against a tree and watched the crew of workers in the cordoned off area checking cables and making last minute adjustments to the array of pyrotechnics. In the middle of it all, seated at a card table in front of a computer console, a woman who looked like a chubby Deadhead ran her finger across the screen with one hand and jabbed at the mouse with the other. Workers occasionally accosted her to ask a question or to show her something. Clearly, she was the person in charge. The woman's aura of authority intrigued Meredith so much that she did not immediately recognize her. In fact, she had to mentally undress her before she realized that, sans her black three-piece suit, the Good Samaritan from the Coon Creek Diner and the fireworks lady were one and the same. Faye.

What had gotten into her? Meredith wondered. Whatever it was, it suited her.

At length, Faye pushed back her chair and cracked her knuckles with satisfaction. She had a paper plate on her lap, and on the plate was a piece of pecan pie with whipped cream. She took a bite with a plastic fork and washed it down with a bottle of hard cider. Meredith decided to stay close and, after the show, introduce herself. Sharing some hard cider and a piece of pie with her seemed like an excellent way to end the day.

When darkness settled, the final speaker of the evening squared himself in front of the podium. "Bless you, friends," he said into the microphone.

"Belvedere! Belvedere! Belvedere!" voices in the crowd shouted.

"Let us pray...." he began.

Spare me your prayers, Meredith thought. Turning her back to him, she watched Faye flip a toggle switch next to her console.

At once, the man of God recoiled from an earsplitting wave of feedback. He tapped at the microphone; it issued a shrill ringing sound that made people cover their ears. Reverend Belvedere tried to speak over the distortion, but the sound swallowed his words. He looked to the sky for a sign. The sound system went dead silent. The spotlights illuminating the stage went dark, and shadows swallowed the reverend.

With a boom, the first firework sped shrieking high into the sky. As it burst above the crowd, music started playing — "Come to My Window" by Melissa Etheridge, of all things. Meredith sang along.

Whatever words the reverend intended to say, he didn't get that opportunity, and although his lips kept moving, nobody listened, nor could they have heard over the fanfare.

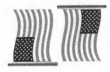

Justin crouched like a sprinter waiting for the starter pistol. He cradled the Boston cream pie in the nook of his arm like a football. He kept a close eye on the stage and checked his watch. The speaker was walking toward the stage, right on time. He started counting down slowly.

Ten one hundred, nine one hundred, eight one hundred...

During his approach, Justin kept his distance by moving through the bushes and tall grasses. Once he nearly tripped over lovers making out on a blanket; the woman laughed and said to him, "Nice looking pie," just as casually as that, even though her bare titties were hanging out.

"Thankee, ma'am," he said respectfully while taking a mental snapshot.

He quickly realized that nobody was paying any attention to him or cared what he was doing, so, curious to see hippies in their natural environment, he altered his path through the crowd. Several people were busy inflating paper bag luminaries in preparation for release. Everywhere, the haze of wacky tobacky was as thick as exhaust from his old man's pickup truck. Justin figured that it wasn't cheating if he got a secondhand buzz, so he snorted every breath for maximum impact. All it did was make his mouth dry. A piece of that pie would taste really good, though.

Seven one hundred, six one hundred, five one hundred....

Despite the many illicit temptations, Justin was resolute. He had a mission. True, he really wanted that tattoo his old man promised to him if he did this. He'd be the envy of the seventh-grade locker room. But his determination went deeper than just that. This was his chance to go down in Coon Creek history, creating a story that father would tell son for generations to come. He'd be as much of a celebrity as Burl Slocum, who ten years after playing high school football was still a hero around town for scoring the winning touchdown against Xenia back in '06. Justin hoped that his deed would merit an equal measure of fame. Maybe he'd even get a girlfriend.

Four one hundred, three one hundred, two one hundred....

A frail old black dude with a funny hat and a colorful shirt that looked like a blanket stepped across a patio and onto the stage. That was his target. "Professor Ass-hole-o," as the Galoots called him. Justin's pa told him that the professor was a terrorist and a communist who hated America. When people in the crowd saw him, they started whooping and hollering, and he raised both arms to embrace their accolades. He stood next to a skinny dude who said he was the common facilitator, or something like that, and accepted a key to the city. Afterwards, the common facilitator stood aside, leaving the spotlight to the professor. He settled in front of the podium and cleared his throat, then said something that sounded like "Asante."

One!

Justin vaulted the steps and flew pie-first across the patio. Professor Ass-hole-o turned to see what was going on.

Splat!

Justin caught the professor full in the face with the Boston cream pie. He gave it a quick turn to smear it into his eyes and up his nose. Then he kept going, off the other side of the patio and into the stunned stillness of the night.

Boom! Fireworks exploded in rapid fire, echoing through the open space. It sounded like a war had broken out in Golden Springs.

People hit the ground. They let go of their luminaries and ran for shelter. The untended sky lanterns slowly wafted above the bedlam. The blasts continued and panic ensued, while tongues of flame ascended heavenward.

Once he was safely away from the fracas, Justin stopped to look back at the chaos he had wrought. *This ought to be worth **two** ass tattoos*, he thought hopefully.

As soon as the first flare sprayed across the sky, the Team of Strangers went to work. As they'd anticipated, Main Street in Coon Creek was bereft of any living soul, save for a drunk passed out in the alley behind a dumpster. Everybody else was at or around the high school stadium to watch the Boom-a-Thon.

Even the Drink Here Tavern had closed for the event. This was their chance to fix history, and in doing so blow off some righteous indignation. El Jefe nailed their manifesto, entitled "Everything You've Been Told Is a Lie," to a tree. It was signed, The Victims.

In the dark, empty park, the statue of Philander Fink looked like it had a worried expression.

"Prepare for your fate," Taara growled at it.

"Are you seriously talking to a statue?" Quang asked, handing her a grappling hook.

"I am savoring the moment," she said as she tied the hooks to the ends of three long ropes.

"Make them tight," El Jefe said. "I don't want one of those hooks to boomerang back at us."

"I tie excellent knots," Taara assured him.

"Where'd you learn that skill?" Quang wanted to know.

"Never you mind."

They stepped back to examine their work. There were three hooks—on a leg, around the hips, and around Philander Fink's neck. Taara tugged on the ropes to satisfy herself that they were secure. Meanwhile, El Jefe twisted the ends of the ropes together and strapped the entire tangle to the trailer hitch on the back of his van.

"This is going to be so cool," Quang said. He took his cell phone out of his pocket and held it in front of himself and the statue in bondage behind him.

"No selfies, you dipshit," El Jefe reprimanded him.

Quang griped, "Spoil sport."

"Everybody get in the van," Taara said.

"I'm riding shotgun," Quang called out.

Before starting the van, the three of them stacked their hands atop each other's and the gearshift. As a team, they shifted into low. El Jefe floored the gas pedal.

In their mental rehearsals, the Team of Strangers had anticipated that the statue of Philander Fink was as spineless as the man himself, and that the force of the van pulling would snap it off its pedestal with the first tug on the ropes. They planned to drag it out of town, then take it to a hole they'd dug in a pasture overlooking the gorge, where they'd bury the evidence and cover the grave with dirt, topped with cow patties.

But the statue stood firm. Inside the van, the Team of Strangers felt an abrupt jolt. At the end of its ropes, the van's tires started spinning, and it began to sway from side to side, but it didn't move an inch forward.

"Fuck me," El Jefe cursed. "I knew this old beater wasn't much stronger than a lawn mower, but I still thought it'd get the job done."

"We will push," Taara said.

She and Quang scampered out of the van and hopped onto the pedestal. Quang put his hands on Philander's butt, and Taara braced herself against his shoulders.

"Now try it," Taara yelled.

Again, El Jefe floored the accelerator. Taara and Quang put all their weight into pushing. Just as before, the van got only as far as the extent of the ropes before it stopped dead in its tracks, like a dog at the end of its leash. The statue creaked, but still resisted.

"Let's try rocking the van," Taara improvised.

El Jefe shifted back and forth repeatedly, while Taara and Quang shoved in time with the vehicle's motion.

"I think I felt it move," Quang said.

"Push harder," Taara ordered.

They put everything they had into one final, Herculean push. The ropes were so taut they hummed. The wheels of the van were burning rubber. The combined forces of push/pull, push/pull built in intensity.

"It's coming," Taara shouted.

At once, Philander Fink's head broke away from its body, bounced off the base of the pedestal, and landed in the grass like a fallen apple.

El Jefe stopped the van and got out. "Fuck me twice," he said.

The Team of Strangers looked at each other, as nonplussed by this turn of events as if their own heads had snapped off.

From a distance, a crescendo of back-to-back fireworks signaled that the grand finale of the Boom-a-Thon was starting.

"Take the head," Taara snapped. "And leave everything else."

"Let's vamos," El Jefe said.

They scrambled into the van and made their getaway, with Taara cradling Philander Fink's head on her lap. When they passed the town limits, El Jefe checked the rearview mirror to see if anybody was following them, then cast a quick backwards glance over his shoulder. He abruptly pulled over to the side of the road.

"What?!?" Quang and Taara blurted.

"Amigos. Look," El Jefe said and pointed.

"Wow," they all said.

The Team of Strangers got out of the van, stood side by side by side, with Taara holding the Fink head, as if so that it could also see, and together they watched in awe as explosions of brilliant colors spread across the sky, forming iridescent bands as they drifted downward. The entire sky seemed to ripple and wave with a glimmering banner.

Mazie pointed the flashlight at a fresh heap of dog turds. "He's gone this way," she deduced.

"How can you tell that it's Shabazz's shit?" Rufus inquired.

"When you walk a dog day after day, you get to know where he likes to shit."

Of course Rufus believed her. Mazie thought that if she told him that Shabazz shat pink eggs, he'd go along with that too. At first, his complaisance had seemed like romantic simplemindedness, which she considered a fatal flaw in writers and boyfriends; but over the past few weeks she'd come to recognize that it was more like an innocent objectivity, a willingness to listen and give her the benefit of doubt, even when doing so strained credulity. There were worse traits in a man.

In reality, despite her insistence, Mazie wasn't sure at all of what she was doing or saying. She was more hopeful than confident.

On their ascent to Shawnee Knob, they heard booming reverberations from Golden Springs. It sounded like the placid little town had become a demilitarized zone.

"That's not good," Rufus said.

"It sounds to me like somebody has sabotaged Independence Day. And I have a pretty good idea who's responsible."

"Oh? Who?"

"Think about it."

Rufus did think about it but seemed to dislike his conclusion. "Really?"

"Duh? Yes."

"I guess we underestimated the ingenuity of rednecks."

"We're all rednecks. We just play on different teams," Mazie said.

Rufus stopped in his tracks, as if that insight was more than he could process while walking at the same time.

Mazie picked up the pace, trying to leave that subject behind them. "Shabazz!" she called.

Rufus, too, shouted, "Shabazz!"

Even in the dark, they covered the trail to Shawnee Knob in half the time they'd normally have taken. As they huffed their way up the final stretch and the clearing came into view, Mazie's doubts clawed to the forefront of her thoughts.

"What if he's not here?" she wondered aloud.

"Don't think ahead of yourself."

"He has to be here, right? You said you knew he'd be here."

"I said that I thought I knew where he was," Rufus clarified. "It was a hunch."

"Shit. If we don't find him here, we'll have to expand the search. I'll go door to door if that's what it takes."

Mazie realized that she loved that stupid dog.

They hustled up the last, steepest part of the trail. Mazie stopped when she felt the ground flatten under her feet. The surrounding forest was so dark as to be featureless, while the open sky above and beyond the clearing was an eerie starless gray. Mazie yielded the lead to Rufus.

"Shabazz!" they both called.

Mazie thought she heard something rustle in the bushes. She listened harder. Then she thought she saw something move among the ferns. She went to look. But there was nothing, just fronds stretching and leaves fluttering. Disappointed, her stomach deflated, and she felt queasy on her feet. She backed up and sat on the bench by the viewpoint, head in hands, wondering what to do next.

She felt something wet brush against the backs of her ankles.

"Shabazz!" Rufus called out triumphantly.

"Where?" Mazie cried.

From under the bench, Shabazz moaned and weakly poked Mazie's legs with his nose.

Rufus pointed his flashlight at them. Huddled beneath the bench, Shabazz and another dog curled around each other, trembling.

"What's this?" Mazie reached down between her legs and rubbed between Shabazz's ears. Not to be ignored, the second dog whimpered and licked Mazie's hand.

"Who are you?" Mazie asked. "And what're you doing hiding under a bench with Shabazz?"

"That's his girlfriend," Rufus answered on behalf of the dog. He lowered himself on one knee and rubbed her neck. "What are you doing here, Dixie?"

Mazie asked for confirmation, "Dixie?"

The beams from two halogen flashlights shone from the far side of the knob, illuminating Mazie, Rufus, and the two dogs like convicts caught in a spotlight. Shielding her eyes, Mazie watched two dark silhouettes—one a behemoth, and the other slight—traipsing through the rubble and brambles, then shimmying through the break in the barbed wire fence. Mazie knew those shadows all too well.

"Shit on toast," she muttered.

Mazie stepped sideways and backwards, leaving Rufus to buffer her from the approaching bodies.

"Who's there?" Rufus called.

The pair advanced into the stark foreground, seeing and being seen at the same time.

Toad, in disbelief: "Mazie?"

Mazie, sheepishly: "Mom?"

Burl, confused: "Mazie?"

Mazie, chagrined: "Burl?"

"Yo, yo, yo," Rufus piped. "Do you guys all know each other?"

Toad pressed her hands against her chest. "My goodness. Mazie. Is it really? How can it be?"

Burl spoke to Mazie: "What in the holy hell are you doing here?" But he was looking at Rufus and sizing him up.

Mazie blinked with fearful clarity, realizing she had nowhere to hide, no plausible excuse, and no face-saving way out that didn't involve confession and begging forgiveness, so, with nothing to lose, she surrendered to willing desperation. She pulled Rufus toward her, wrapped her arms over his shoulders, and smacked a hot, wet kiss on his lips.

Rufus liquefied in her arms, drenched with arousal, soggy with gratitude. It felt to Mazie like the only thing holding him up was the linkage between their mouths, and if she let go, he'd spill into a puddle on the ground in front of her. She embraced him tighter and supported him upright by sliding one leg between his. She wanted to make this moment last at least long enough for her to figure out how she was going to explain herself.

Mazie heard her mother say, "Mazie, darling. What in the heck are you doing? Who's that? And Dixie! Oh, Dixie. I can't believe this. It's like I'm dreaming."

Mazie slowly peeled back from Rufus. His puzzled gaze lingered over her. She felt like she was in the spotlight of a million contradictions, without a single good answer for anybody.

Rufus started to ask, "What—"

Mazie stifled him by pressing a finger against his lips. She wasn't ready to answer that question. Nor was she ready to answer the questions she expected from the others. She stood looking at the ground.

The next few seconds passed in a jumbled cacophony of everybody talking in monosyllables over everybody else.

"I don't get it—"

"What in the—"

"How did you—"

"Who—"

"Why—"

"What—"

"Can somebody please—"

Shabazz and Dixie got the last word, though. In the confusion, the amorous canines snuck out from under the bench and padded, side by side, to the viewpoint; they barked together, as if to say, "Shut up and look."

Rufus stepped away from the verbal melee and faced the open sky. He called back to friends, lovers, and strangers alike: "You guys. Come here. You've got to see this."

Four humans and two dogs stood beside each other in enthralled silence. To the south, high above Golden Springs, dozens of paper luminaries floated like lucent ghosts in a gently spiraling pattern that unfurled across the valley. Farther, to the north, the aerial spectacle of the Coon Creek fireworks show was entering its grand finale. The volley of successive missiles soared high enough to look like comets at the peak of their trajectory, then burst, one by one, into multicolored layers that blended together as they descended to form a broad arching rainbow flag of violet over blue over green over yellow over orange over red, stretching from horizon to horizon.

"Now there's something you don't see every day," Rufus commented.

Mazie stood with Rufus to her right and her mother to her left. She dreaded the questions that she knew were coming, once the fireworks were over. Then a notion popped into her head like a bombshell. The easiest thing to do was simply tell the truth. All of it. It was worth a try. What's the worst that could happen?

For the moment, though, none of that mattered. She envisioned her friends and family—and all of the good people in Coon Creek, as well as Golden Springs— all looking toward the sky with reverence—minds blown, jaws hanging, eyes bulging, hearts racing, oohing and aahing, and, in that instant, everyone feeling downright neighborly.

Hi. Nothing helps an unknown writer more than a reader's rating on Amazon, Goodreads, etc. Thanks

ABOUT THE AUTHOR

Gregg Sapp, a native Ohioan, is a Pushcart Prize-nominated writer, librarian, college teacher and academic administrator. He is the author of the "Holidazed" series of satires, each of which is centered around a different holiday. The first two novels, *Halloween from the Other Side* and *The Christmas Donut Revolution* were published in 2019 by Evolved Publishing. Previous books include *Dollarapalooza* (Switchgrass Books, 2011) and *Fresh News Straight from Heaven* (Evolved Publishing, 2018), based upon the life and folklore of Johnny Appleseed. He has published humor, poetry, and short stories in Defenestration, Waypoints, Semaphore, Kestrel, Zodiac Review, Top Shelf, Marathon Review, and been a frequent contributor to Midwestern Gothic, and others. Gregg lives in Tumwater, WA.

For more, please visit Gregg Sapp online at:
Website: www.SappGregg.net
Goodreads: Gregg Sapp
Twitter: @Sapp_Gregg
Facebook: Gregg.Sapp.1
LinkedIn: Gregg-Sapp-b515921b

WHAT'S NEXT?

Gregg is fast at work on the next book in the
"Holidazed" series, and other books will follow that,
so please stay tuned to his page at our website to
remain up to date:
www.EvolvedPub.com/GSapp

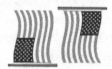

Indeed, the best way to be assured that you won't miss
important developments is to subscribe to our
newsletter here:
www.EvolvedPub.com/Newsletter

MORE FROM GREGG SAPP

Don't miss Gregg Sapp's award-winning adult tale of
an American icon, Johnny Appleseed.

FRESH NEWS STRAIGHT FROM HEAVEN

*"I happen to believe that genius makes people weird," a
storyteller once said, explaining how Johnny Appleseed
could be at once so peculiar and so profound.*

Between 1801 and 1812, Ohio and the Old Northwest
territory runs wild and brutal, with a fragile peace, savage
living conditions, and the laws of civilization far away.
Still, settlers stake everything they own on the chance of
building better lives for themselves in this new frontier.

John Chapman--aka Johnny Appleseed--knows this
land better than any white man. Everywhere he goes, he
shares the "Fresh News Straight from Heaven," which
he hears right from the voices of angels who chat with
him regularly. God had promised him personally that
he could build peace by growing fruit.

Convincing people of that vision, though, is no
easy task. Most folks consider him mad.

This land teems with a miscellaneous assemblage of
soldiers, scoundrels, freebooters, runaway slaves, circuit
riders, and religious cultists. Ambitious politicians, like

Aaron Burr and William Henry Harrison, dream of creating a new empire there. Meanwhile, a reformed drunkard emerges among the Shawnee as a Prophet, one who spoke with the Great Spirit, Waashaa Monetoo. Along with his brother, the war chief Tecumseh, the Prophet begins building an Indian coalition to take back their land.

Even while the tensions mount, Johnny, with angels urging him on, skates blithely through the crossfire and turmoil, spreading his message, impervious to the mockery and derision being heaped upon him. Finally, however, his faith is challenged when war breaks out in the land, leading to the bloody battle of Tippecanoe between Harrison's army and the Shawnee Prophet's warriors, and ultimately to the declaration of the War of 1812. A violent massacre near the northern Ohio town of Mansfield leaves its citizens terrified and vulnerable.

In a desperate act of faith, Johnny promises the people that he can save them. Thus, he dashes off on a midnight run, seeking to spread peace across a land on the brink of war. With so many lives at stake, Johnny must confront the ultimate test of his convictions.

MORE FROM EVOLVED PUBLISHING

We offer great books across multiple genres, featuring high-quality editing (which we believe is second-to-none) and fantastic covers.

As a hybrid small press, your support as loyal readers is so important to us, and we have strived, with tireless dedication and sheer determination, to deliver on the promise of our motto: **QUALITY IS PRIORITY #1!**

Please check out all of our great books, which you can find at this link:
www.EvolvedPub.com/Catalog/

Thank you!

CPSIA information can be obtained
at www.ICGtesting.com
Printed in the USA
FSHW021552200620
71374FS